A BRIEF ALPHABET
OF TORTURE

A BRIEF ALPHABET OF TORTURE

STORIES

VI KHI NAO

FC2
TUSCALOOSA

FC2 is an imprint of the University of Alabama Press

Inquiries about reproducing material from this work should be addressed to the University of Alabama Press

Book Design: Publications Unit, Department of English, Illinois State University; Director: Steve Halle, Production Assistant: Sarah Lyons
Cover Design: Lou Robinson

Typeface: Garamond

The author gratefully acknowledges the following journals in which stories in *A Brief Alphabet of Torture: Stories* first appeared, sometimes in slightly different form: *NOON*, *Hobart*, *SmokeLong Quarterly*, *Mud Season Review*, and *alice blue*.

Library of Congress Cataloging-in-Publication Data

Names: Nao, Vi Khi, 1979- author.
Title: A brief alphabet of torture : stories / Vi Khi Nao.
Description: Tuscaloosa : FC2, [2017]
Identifiers: LCCN 2017005462 (print) | LCCN 2017010987 (ebook) | ISBN
  9781573660617 (softcover) | ISBN 9781573668729 (Ebook)
Classification: LCC PS3614.A63 A6 2017 (print) | LCC PS3614.A63 (ebook) | DDC
  813/.6--dc23
LC record available at https://lccn.loc.gov/2017005462

for Hồ Xuân Hương

CONTENTS

A BRIEF ALPHABET OF TORTURE

I

THIGHS OF NYMPHS

MAGNOLIA, AMBROSIO, VALANCE stand still as three pillars. Among the ruins of the Roman Empire. Cows gathering like daffodils. They have been behaving well. With their collars up. They stand like authentic marble blocks.

They learn how to build good relationships with math. To respect their neighbors' space. Their neighbors will remark that they have been frying salmon with salt in their apartment. They will complain that the three pillars have stunk up their cardigans and their new button-down blouses. Their strapless dresses. Their drawstring pants.

But Valance and Ambrosio and Magnolia are not children anymore. Despite the shift in maturity. They still behave poorly.

They fry tilapia over the skillet, trap the smell inside of sweaters and blouses and socks, and refuse to eat dirt properly. Though they apparently seem to speak quite properly.

For instance, they spend an enormous amount of time outdoors. Instead, they spend an indecent amount indoors.

Their meeting is cumbersome.

VALANCE: Will you trap something for me?

AMBROSIO: Your choice of fish?

VALANCE: Walleye. (*She hesitates.*)

AMBROSIO: It won't work. It is hardly toxic enough. (*He states firmly.*)

MAGNOLIA: Grouper.

AMBROSIO: Halibut.

VALANCE: I don't know what to say.

AMBROSIO: I insist. If you have an intense distaste for this neighbor, halibut will do the job. Yes, a halibut sandwich.

VALANCE: The neighbor lives on the fourth floor. (*Silence.*)

VALANCE: Pretend you are catering to a crowd of twenty-five individuals. With olfactory issues.

AMBROSIO: Twenty-five sandwiches? Do you think that is a bit much?

VALANCE: Hamlet hasn't stopped being a nuisance ever since he moved in. First, he asks to borrow my blender. And later, he comes by around four in the afternoon, usually, and requests for a toilet plunger. It doesn't ever stop. Fry some fish and see if he will move away.

Ω

So it's settled.

Before the halibut can be tossed into a skillet, Ambrosio and Valance and Magnolia and another young man named Mr. Table arrive promptly at one of Valance's upscale apartments. It is inevitable they must move the furniture. First, they move the sofas into the huge U-Haul rental truck. They stack books into boxes. And carry down the coffee table. They take the chairs stacked inside the closet and relocate them down from the third floor. They lift the bed frames. The mattresses. And the dinning table. The enormous idiot box. The curtains. Curtains. Removed. Stored into laundry baskets. They empty all of her closets. They set a game of monopoly on the floor. Each time they move an item, they roll a dice. If they land in jail, it is break time. They often do not go to jail. They do not break. And on their way downstairs with boxes of porcelain dishes and tchotchkes, they purchase two hotels on Broadway. They purchase quite a few railroad companies. Their trains are in good business. People are paying a fee. Their move begins on Friday. But it takes them a week to move out.

By next Saturday, Ambrosio is standing at her stove—

In a dismally bare apartment. He is frying halibut. When he fries the halibut, he opens the apartment doors wide. In fact, he hauls a standing fan into the apartment to reroute and to blow the redolent halibut closer to the fourth floor. When the standing fan is dispersing down to all levels of the apartment, he breaks down the commercial fan and purchases five industrial fans that lie on the ground, low, like snipers. At Lowe's, he purchases 150 feet of lightweight aluminum pipe. Ten inches in diameter. He runs the pipe down to the fourth floor of the apartment. The pipe's orifice faces the front door of the neighbor. Pleased with his effort, Ambrosio in his green apron, begins the enormous feat. Olive oil poured in the skillet. The skillet on low heat. He tosses the halibut slowly into it. He watches the oil flicker and jump out of the skillet, like spitting fish. He keeps his eye on the fans as they attempt to convey the pungent smell of the virgin oil sea through the pipe.

The aluminum spatula resting on the kitchen counter catches Ambrosio's attention. He notices a distorted version of a fat woman's face undulating on the surface of the spatula.

A hand pounds on the open door. Ambrosio turns the oven to a lower temperature. He rubs his hands on his apron and walks to the door entrance to see who is bright enough to disturb him.

NEIGHBOR: Hello. (*The neighbor, in a white apron, stands outside of his door. His forehead is profusely diaphoretic. With one of his hands on his hip, he reaches with the other to greet Ambrosio. The two men exchange a brief, tight handshake.*)

AMBROSIO: Hello neighbor.

NEIGHBOR: You are looking? (*The neighbor stares at his green apron and smiles in jest at the remarkable sentinel at the door.*)

AMBROSIO: I am certainly not looking.

NEIGHBOR: I am. (*His gaze fixed steadily on Ambrosio.*)

AMBROSIO: What are you looking?

NEIGHBOR: I am looking for a spatula to lift pork out of my iron pan. Apparently, it went missing. (*His empty hand lifts up to mirror the content of his speech.*)

AMBROSIO: That is a hitch.

NEIGHBOR: It doesn't appear that way.

AMBROSIO: It does. (*Ambrosio is slightly tetchy.*)

NEIGHBOR: Do you have a spatula?

AMBROSIO: I am frying halibut with it. I am afraid that it does suggest that I do have one.

NEIGHBOR: In that case, I am inclined towards your spatula. May I just borrow it to lift my pork? I will return it to you in a—in a blink. A blimp. A zilch. Like nothing.

AMBROSIO: I am sorry to decline you. But you may not, may not, gravitate toward my spatula. It is apparently occupied.

The neighbor dashes into the kitchen passing just by Ambrosio's hair by half an inch, who stands guarding the door. Ambrosio runs after him. The neighbor spots the spatula supine on the kitchen counter. On his way out of the kitchen, the neighbor dodges past Ambrosio by one-fourth of an inch. Ambrosio, the spatula aegis, fails to behave religiously and accordingly. He is a snail, trapped between a hare and an elephant.

AMBROSIO: You will contaminate my spatula! You pork! I demand it back. (*Yelling at the top of his lungs.*)

NEIGHBOR: I promise you will have it back.

He sprints out of Valance's apartment and disappears down the stairs. Fear drives him back into the kitchen. He returns to the kitchen and stares at the skillet. His halibut needs to be flipped, but there is no spatula. He turns the oven off and lifts the skillet into the sink. He turns cold water on it. Half of the exposed cheeks whiten. Whiten. Whiten. Alabaster like the thighs of nymphs. Water nymphs. He regrets that he is not a minnow.

DOING AN EVA HESSE ON A MAN

SHE HAS BEEN ON THE PHONE over an hour thinking about the sound of the shower running. She thinks that it is raining on the other side of the wall or rather on the other side of the line. But nothing that interesting ever happens to her during a tedious conversation, and certainly not during a conversation about a rebate on a phone she has recently purchased. She keeps on telling herself that another minute, just another and another and another and then fifty doors, no fifty dollars, will be sent to her mailing address. The man on the phone insists that she stay on the phone. He insists that he must take a shower first before continuing the debate. My office has a shower, he adds. She nods her head in approval. She nods. But he doesn't know that she has nodded. On the phone, she whispers, I am nodding. Are you listening? But she hears the sound of water tapping. Meanwhile, she is on the last drop of her patience. Hello? Are you there? The hoarse voice of a man comes through the other line. She waits a moment in disbelief. She thinks that he has left his shower running. Running. When his voice comes through, it startles her. She isn't ready for a human being to talk to her about the rebate. She was expecting a shower. The rain. She misses the rain. Yes. Long pause. I am here. She says, Hello. Hello. Are you dressed? Yes, I am dressed, he replies. I can't offer you the debate you want. I don't know what to say and I am not really good at convincing others. No. No. No. I meant I wanted my rebate for a recently purchased phone. I don't have a debate for your phone. I am sorry, woman. Don't let me go! She shrieks. She has waited for over an hour for her rebate. He is unable to hang up on her. The shriek jolts him awake. He calculates the consequences of hanging up on her. She thinks for a moment and asks him if he has seen Eva Hesse's sculpture called *Hang Up*? He clears his throat to answer and she restarts the dialogue on her rebate. He presses the phone to his ears. What debate, lady? He asks. What? He wants to run his shower again. Return to it, at least. But her shriek haunts him. Together they cling to the phones. Strangers clinging to one another. Broken. You can ride me if you like? She hesitantly offers. Ride you what, he repeats? The phone. The awful phone. Does it ever translate right? Does it? The debate. What does she wish to debate about, he thinks? He considers various topics running through his mind. Before he can get anywhere with his thinking, he halts. And reaches for the phone. How about Eva Hesse? He knows nothing of Eva, but he is ready to debate her. There is silence on the other end. She hasn't responded to him. He begins to worry when the silence is extended. Eva Hesse, he whispers. Finally, a voice rings through. Eva Hesse knows nothing about my rebate. She is dead. Do you know? She is dead. Died of a brain tumor. She won't be able to help me. Can't you understand? But he does understand her. She will only be dead temporarily, he attempts to articulate his argument. Some people, he begins, do not die all the way through. They get giddy and grow tired of dying so they never make it all the way through. Couldn't she see that he was making a valiant effort? I do understand you, he says. I do understand you, he repeats. I am getting to know her even better and better. She thinks he is losing it. And that is charming. You are charming, she declares over the phone. Show me what you got? I have nothing. I got a debate going. Do not send my rebate to some stranger! Okay? I don't want it to be at some random address. Are you writing down my address? I am giving it to you for the umpteenth time. I am getting sick of repeating my address to you. Shall I do an Eva Hesse on you? Oh please, don't hang up on me, he begs. I can take a second shower. Or a third, he offers. He thinks she is capable of accepting his second shower. Okay, she replies. Go shower. Over the phone, she hears the tapping of rain. The shower is running. And he is in it. She hangs up on him. She has to. The time has come. When she is far from the phone, she throws herself off the balcony. Into the swimming pool. Closer to rain, she thinks. He picks up the phone. He hears nothing. Not even a buzzer. Absolutely nothing. And the man in the shower sits by the phone, waiting endlessly for her to come through the other line. He waits and he waits. Sitting by the phone, waiting.

I LOVE YOU ME NEITHER

I HAVE JUST RUSHED IN from the exact zero degrees outside shuffling snow. The snow sparkled and shimmered like a
white lake. It was a gorgeous evening to be outside. And cold!
I like the raw air of December (not really for its extreme bleakness) that cuts through my skin like a dream through the spirit,
and I love the way I can't feel my toes. They are like a glob of
cold clay. Sometimes I feel them so alienated from the rest of my
body that it seems as if they could talk to me like another friend.
My friend, Tony, did not come to work today. On his way from
Cedar Rapids, he ran into a ditch. The extreme cold must have
broken the asphalt floor. I am just glad he did not get run over.
You would like Tony if you were to meet him. He is a rough boy.
There is a prominent German feature about him. He is rather

mild, but at times reticent. Do not trust that he is shy or mellow. For he is neither of those. Pay particular attention to his shoes. I have just come in from the cold. The night before, Wednesday, he had generously dropped me off. I don't know what it is about that evening that drowned a mortal part of me. As he pulled right into my parking lot, "I Love You Me Neither" was blasting from his Volvo's speakers. It was about an orgasm. In Tony's black Volvo, the hush and moan and groan of a woman's voice vibrated gently, rocking it like a vessel in the sea of pavement and grass and snow. He shifted the gear into park. This was an extrapolation of the driving existence: in stalling mode. The heat of the moan and groan contrasted strangely, almost bewilderingly, against the stoic barrenness of subzero climate. The glissando of the song increased in tempo. I thought of Tony, who slouched in the driver's seat. He looked abysmally contented, perhaps he'd lost himself in the eternal reminiscence, perhaps replaying in his mind the love-making scenes of holding Neo, his orgasm, waiting, with permission from her for the release—mimicking the lyrical content of the song. And where was I in this black Volvo? Reconstructing the pillars of passion? I wasn't contemplating much—just the fact that we sat there in front of my parking lot as we listened to the song in its last moments of closure. I felt the absence and the complete presence of self as it attempted to absorb the subterranean air of the orgasm. In the side mirror, gas ushered itself from the exhaust, and the cold air contained the fumes in their moments of escape. Like a sheet of smoke. Frozen precipitation danced behind the back bumper. I slumped in the passenger seat, exhaling and inhaling the silk fabric of cold air and thought nothing of love, sex, or mortality. I thought of zilch. What was it about listening to a pseudo-orgasm in a black Volvo that made me feel like my heart was a bird whose wings had been clipped off, or a balloon, inflating and deflating, and I was waiting, waiting for it to pop? And it never popped! I slumped in the passenger seat, because—my mind's incapacity perhaps—I couldn't imagine an orgasm of that caliber to truly exist. It seemed so nearly improbable. Glissando. Glissando. Glissando. Intimacy is…pseudo, and, well, full of betrayal. It's only loyal to itself and hardly ever considers its transient traits, of which it possesses many. Intimacy is a bird with beautiful, fragile, white wings and as time passes, they fall off feather by feather. They defoliate like leaves. When intimacy is in existence, basically dead, it's nothing but a useless bird, it's even silly to think it could fly. It can't go anywhere. And I think now, in retrospect, that perhaps the real extraordinary postmodern orgasm is the one that happened in the black Volvo, a voice of a woman who moaned and groaned—while Tony and I sat silently in prayer, praying that the syncopated cries that banged against the car windows had not mistaken our hearts for our pants. We relived in that moment a sincere quasi-intimacy of some sort through the voice of a woman, anonymous to me, who can't and couldn't vocalize in any other way but to simply send her hoarse, sexy groans out to a car sitting in between glasses, banging her vocal orifice into the night's mysterious ecstasy. The windows chattered. And I felt like melting into wax, into a molded cone. I felt like losing myself. If I could place that experience with Tony, it would fit in the following abstraction: Imagine Tony's Volvo as a black box. Imagine my parking lot as a dot in outer space. The rest of the space is white. And imagine nothing else exists.

Imagine a woman's orgasm ripped the box open. She walked out and evaporated. Tony's shoes flapped like a fragile bird and my nipples were steamed. In the cold. Behind many layers of wool.

THE BALD SPARROW

USING ONLY ONE HAND, the professor cradles his penis like a fat old man carrying a sparrow up a mountain. His over-sized oxford shirt drapes his thighs. He holds his penis gently but firmly, without suffocating it, while he talks to his student about her latest story, in which she wrote about a confused daughter who accidentally suffocates her mother to death in New Guinea. There is a desk between the professor and the student, blocking her from seeing what the professor is doing with his left hand. There is an eye peeping through the keyhole, another student's, as it happens, the best writer in the program, and even he cannot see what the professor is up to. But the narrator can see, can see exactly what the professor is doing, which is the only sight that matters in the revision of a narration that is about to happen or has already happened.

"So, how are you going to make it more feasible for the daughter to 'accidentally' suffocate her mother?"

The professor emphasizes the word "accidentally" by rotating his jaw to the far left of his cheekbone and then counter-rotating it to the far right before licking his parched lips. It's very early in the afternoon. Though his back is to the window, the skin of his lips has become desiccated, giving the illusion that his mouth is a baked potato sliced in half, self-peeling without him knowing. He smacks his lips as the student responds. The sound of his smacking eats one and a quarter words from the student's mouth.

"ughter is fat!"

The professor leans forward.

"What did you say?"

"I said 'The daughter is fat!'"

"And...?"

The professor leans further forward.

"She sat on her mother."

"And you expect the reader to believe that an adult can sit on another adult as an act of murder?"

"Yes. Especially since the mother is very thin, a strip of noodle, and the daughter is very fat like the national park."

He leans back in his chair.

"You can be a thief of reality all you want, as long as you get away with it. As your teacher of sound narrative and gatekeeper of logic, I see you robbing reality and I am stopping you from robbing it."

"How?"

"How what?"

"How are you going to stop me?"

"By asking you to revise. By giving you a poor grade."

The professor, whose makeshift-paperweight arm pins the manuscript solidly to the desk, is startled when in one swift maneuver the student pulls the manuscript from beneath his arm and shoves it into her fake-Gucci backpack.

"I'm not finished grading it yet," the professor raises his voice while crushing his sparrow. He has been so good at being gentle with it, petting it as he ascends the mountain of his student's logical home.

"You are now."

If his hand were not inside his pants, cradling his artificially enlarged and modified sparrow, he would have demanded her manuscript back through physical exertion—though, more accurately, his preferred noun is "force." Through sheer force. He imagines climbing on top of his desk, his pants kissing the wood, while he commands her to walk towards him and turn around. In the pornographic world, he would command her to drop her skirt and her cherry underpants and bend over while he fucks her in the ass. In his substandard office, he imagines taking his sparrow and placing it first on her right shoulder and then over her head and down onto her left shoulder. As if his sparrow were a sword and he were making his student into a knight, not a writer. A knight of his own desire. He opens his mouth like Madonna and sings "Like A Virgin."

Over truffles and tortellini once, his knees had bumped lightly against hers. He had kept them there, not breathing, not moving out of fear of losing the connection. They were in a bar; she was visiting the department, not yet a student. In the light, he could see how beautiful she was. Her long black Nordic hair swung back and forth like the pendulum of a Wildon Home grandfather clock. He had ached to pull her hair over, either to stop the swing of time or to forward it, to a time when he could lean over and kiss her and make her blush. Soon enough, he would be her teacher and thesis advisor. They would sip Mariage Frères while chewing on a madeleine and talking about Marcel Proust.

She was a strong writer. She frequently wrote about cephalopod mollusks that could grant wishes by squirting ink. In one story, she had written, "If you spread your leg, the octopus suggests, I will inseminate you with black desire and the next time you pee, you will pee out your future." She would write about prophecies from the point of view of an eggplant. He would be absurd, ask her to make her realism more realistic. He would encourage frequent visits, but she would only meet him the minimum required amount: three times per semester. He keeps lurching for her longcase, but it keeps swinging out of reach.

She is a talented writer, but the school has many talented writers. The professor is quite aware of this. His longcase student hasn't been performing at her best. She has been drifting in and out of depression from her terrible marriage with her Flying Spaghetti Monster husband, and her ability to perform has decreased drastically. But when the time comes for the university's annual writing competition, she too submits. It is the Seiichi Morimura Prize, named after the Japanese mystery writer born in Kumagaya, and it carries an award of ten thousand dollars. Morimura donated to the university part of his earnings for his successful and controversial work, *The Devil's Gluttony*.

The professor reads the submissions with his hand cradling his sparrow and when he reaches hers, he masturbates profusely, rubbing his sparrow's feathers until it is nearly bald. Like her one-legged octopus, he squirts his ink onto the first page of her manuscript and makes all the characters' dreams come true. He resurrects the spaghetti-thin mother from the grave her daughter gave her. The process makes him feel empowered, like a superhero saving imaginary characters from their tragic fates. He selects her work blindly, above all others. He speaks to the other professors, raving about her extraordinary talent and her amazing matricidal story.

It is a Wednesday when he comes bursting into the main office to see the result of the competition. The best writer in the program is standing by the coffee maker, pouring himself another cup of coffee.

"Professor Humblebee! Would you like a cup of coffee?"

The professor ignores the student. Noticing a manila envelope sitting near the mailbox, he bends his body over the locked swinging door of the main office to reach for it. But he is one index-finger-length short. The secretary, Helen, sits with her nose glued to the typewriter.

"Hey Helen, would you pass me the result?"

Standing up, she gives him the envelope, "You are in early!"

He ignores Helen too and pulls the paper out of the envelope, like pulling hair from a skull, smiles, then shoves the paper back in. He whistles. The student with the cup of coffee has been observing all of this. He too had entered the competition.

His story wasn't one of matricide. He wrote, instead, about a colored soldier from the Civil War era who devoted his remaining amputated days to writing about his experience in the war. He had collected the teeth of deceased soldiers and chiseled them down so he could turn the teeth into braille for his blind sweetheart. He narrated beautifully, the experience of her running her hands through the calcified manuscript, sensing the ghosts of the war and the memories of the soldiers passing through the tips of her fingers. She could feel the materiality of their war efforts. The story concluded with his visually impaired lover asking him to pull out one of her wisdom teeth and use it to compose the last footnote of his autobiographical account of the war. When she died, he pulled out the rest of her teeth and wrote her an epithet in braille and mounted it on her headstone. He knew he was writing at his height and he had worked hard, day and night, for that prize. He knew from Humblebee's smile that he had no chance.

A few months ago, Daphne had come in secret to his one-bedroom apartment on top of a hill, sobbing to him that Humblebee had attempted to kiss her. She had dodged his parched lips. She said she had been afraid to come to the program because she had a bad feeling something like this would happen. He didn't know what to say to her. From the prize earnings he had received from a Hemingway Award, he ordered this Nordic girl mee katang, amok trey, a large bowl of kuy teav, num banh chok, kdam chha mrich kchei, chruok svay, samlar kair, pleah sach ko, and ansom chek from the Cambodian restaurant down the street. He couldn't understand how she could eat all of that food in one sitting and still remain who she was. Tall and beautiful. Not like him. He has the slowest metabolism in the world.

He had been fat all his life, but he wrote well and it compensated for his lack of Ryan Gosling looks. When he saw Professor Humblebee from the corner of his eye as he poured the blackest coffee into a cup, he understood. He was an astute observer and he could see through Humblebee's academic lust, could see that even if he had written like James Joyce or William Faulkner at their height, he wouldn't have had a chance.

Daphne slowly drifted out of his life. At a bakery once, he saw her sitting across from a young man with a big beer belly and a massive mustache an inch longer than Dali's. He didn't think she saw him, and quietly he sneaked away three almond biscotti and one large chocolate chip cookie tucked inside the pockets of his gray hoodie.

A few summers after graduation: he is walking with a pencil and a small notepad in his pocket on a flat, dry field toward a mulberry tree. Three or four yards from him a cairn, a beautiful sculpture shaped like a round pyramid, sits handsomely in the sun. He thought he saw a Sudan golden sparrow, but closer inspection shows that the golden light of the afternoon has played a trick on him. It is just a house sparrow and like most sparrows, it has fallen in love with the dust. Dust bathing is the most common hobby that sparrows engage in. Here, the young passerine dips its beak down, tail in the air, while digging a hole with its feet. As soon as it has completed its plowing task, the bird lies down in the hole and flaps its wings. Hunter immediately walks away from the gravedigger and towards the cairn. He removes one average-sized stone, the size of a human palm, and walks back to the hole. The light that is reflecting on his back has the same golden tone as the light that fell on the professor's back the afternoon he critiqued Daphne's paper. Hunter bends his knees so when the base of this foot stretches and arches like his leather sandal, he is prostrating before the bird, the tip of the pencil digging into his thigh, giving him a small pain that could be compared to pleasure. He holds the stone in his right hand, gripping its side with all five of his fingers. He holds the stone probably not in the same way that Agave held her son Pentheus's impaled head before presenting it to Cadmus. And in one swift move he collapses the shadow created by the stone lifting, and gives the sparrow's bird-made, dirt-designed burial chamber the lid it deserves.

II

SUICIDE BOMBER

ROWING A TINY BOAT, I THOUGHT I could reach the hem of the horizon. Rowing under it would not be a dream come true. Rowing along the side of the hem is not cream nor nightmare nor October. When it loses its breath to a stem dying on its own pithy soil. What it is like to see oil while you are rowing your boat, where the sun matters most as it spills God's miscarriage or adultery. You skin your rug because it has come from an (animal fainting) fainting animal + you skin your ironing board because you have made a mistake. You burn your fabric. You burn your table while you row your tiny boat + the oil on the surface of the sea gazes at you as if you were the breeze that has lost its ardor to row. When you reach the hem of the horizon, it is not what you think it is: not your mother ceasing swaying. It's your father, un-deflated, blowing backwards into his lungs a helium balloon, which you mistake for the evaporating sky, the opposite of a sunrise. When you rise in the morning, you are full again. The content of your soul is not made (entirely) of strobing sunlight stroked by an ashtray. The content of your soul is made (entirely) of detergent + snow, which spill over the fire escape because you live in an apartment complex inside of a timer's body, which tells you when to live, when to die, when to row your boat + when to explode.

A CHILD'S FACE HAS BEEN PICKPOCKETED BY TERRORISTS

THE TRAIN FRONT AND BACK. To push Syrian children through the threshold of weaponized cyanide. Soporific-shaped children line forever on tiles in eastern Ghouta and the moaning comes from a small hut in a British bush by a woman spreading wide for a man and later wider for a woman. There are times like this where a nonexistent page whispers to another page: at the corridor of your dildo, my cunt turns around in reluctance and walks quietly into a field of pubic hair and a field of amputated hands. You are sprawled out, vulnerable to my finger that runs along your English skin, a partition between the Assad milieu and your river of red hemoglobin. Above, the sun keeps on rising while the eastern border whimpers a little, a little into the skin of fog. Your crater of a mouth. Words collecting spigots of air and hair and this immortal note you had called breathing. Breathe you say. Breathe. Not even to a makeshift hospital. You said that you were to dye your hair blond for me so that when I fucked you in the middle of the night, it would seem as if I was yanking the sun out of you so that part of your scalp was not present and my hand fainting on the hair belonged to no one. You shake a little. You said this because you thought, uprooting strands of human beauty, a response to the crisis in the Middle East would make you feel less in exile. Someone walks out of a pleasure room and whispers to you, "You are a boy and I am not a girl." Your patch of hairless scalp: an over-shaved moon on the universe, which is your face. You turn your face towards me. You are no longer afraid of highland and lowland, after all, a child's face in Damascus has just been pickpocketed by the impact of human meteorites.

A BLANKET
OF SARCOPHAGI

BERLIN AND I HAVE HAD TO INHALE the desert whose arms and legs lengthen as we walk. We have not been walking long, and dry sand leaks from the bottoms of our feet while the air surrounds us like confessional knives. Behind or above us, Jerusalem or America. Not long ago, and then, my lungs, Berlin said, are heavy with dark fluids and I don't know if I have the energy to cross the sea of sand with you, Mansion. And I think it's dark, this bed full of waterless air that blooms while Berlin's dry mouth opens behind the Judean hills. We walk slowly, Berlin. One foot over the other foot. I am sorry our faces are peeling off, Berlin. We are only tiny tangerines. Berlin's curly hair flops back into the mattress of sand. The days pass like the pages of the past. The wind arrives with dehydrating tasks and sometimes

Berlin's skirt lives outside of Jerusalem and has to walk back to Berlin's body and Mansion's blouse travels like an uncle through a clan of nomads. It's so hard, you know, Mansion, when darkness presses on your skin while the shirt you wear won't iron your soul. You know it's hard to walk away from the Holy City with bags of sand bundled like newborn calves beneath my calves. I want to tell Berlin that we do not have to be Moses and talk to God and we do not have to kill an Egyptian and hide him in the sand. Our task is very simple...all we are obliged and destined to do is to lift this one page made of miles and miles of biblical eyes and mouths off the Holy Desert and see what lies beneath. Not too far from us, the windless wind turns the pages of Berlin's Bible like a switchblade. Berlin delivers her words, Mansion, I wish we brought our banana leaf sleeping bags with us. I wish that too, Berlin. I wish we were sleeping beneath a banana tree and in my sleep I would make you a sleeping bag from the arms of the banana tree.

IN A SEXUAL SLANG

THIS MORNING I WOKE UP with a bladder full of magnets and petroleum. Parts of me are magnetized to heliotrope, which refers to heliotropium, and made me think of floral petroleum. The other parts of me are craving an extremely sanitized asshole and a microphone. Centuries ago, the ancients wouldn't have guessed that the human asshole can be used as a hydrocarbon pipeline. This, and getting blown up from the inside and becoming a half-mourning periorbital flower, not from war, but from peace. When the petroleum left my body somebody once compared the departure to an Ethiopian exodus. I find myself walking slowly in a sexual slang towards the Gaza Strip. A woman who pinned my soul down told me I could pull a sofa over near where the sea wept and sip *qamar deen* and I could taste the entire Koran that way for sure. Sitting in that living room, all the Palestinians smell like chicken broth. Now that my body is no longer a prisoner of gas pipes, my stomach can be a pillowcase filled with unsalted goat cheese. Later I will talk to my even-toed, wild Bactrian ungulate named Hummus bi Tahini. He has a beautiful asshole. I had him imported from the Gobi Desert. We survived several sandstorms together before Saudi Arabia inserted one gas pipeline through my asshole. One friend asked me if I was a gas station.

MY WIFE'S EARS
AND NOSE

THE HOURS OF DISBELIEF rush me to hold myself at the center. I have been holding myself together. These long months. These ridiculous, silly years. There are times like this when cutting my wife's ears and nose wasn't enough. She kept on dishonoring me in ridiculously silly ways, dishonoring my manhood, dishonoring my family, and my mother won't stop complaining about her. She would return anyway and of course, you know how silly it is for a wife to leave her husband. And my penis would ache, like these terrible moans at nights, with stiffness and disorientation. I would inhale and consider all things possible, what I would do to her. My family would approve. My mother, in particular. Often times, my friends would ask: well, how did you cut them off? Did you wait until she fell asleep? Did you drug her? Did she struggle? Of course she struggled, thrashing about and I had to pin her down like a ravaged animal. She was wide-awake for it! And with a kitchen knife I hacked her first ear off and before she realized what was happening to her, I forced her face to turn the other direction, like how betrayal is the symbol of love, I hacked her other ear like cutting a bull's ear off after a bullfight. Cutting her nose was harder, pinching her nose for grip wasn't the most natural exercise. It was the altitude of her nose too. It was a predicament. The crunchy bone tissue. There are these amazing ways in which as the head of the household I have to consider, for my family's sake and for my future's sake. My life has drawn long like a water pipe and these small rivers that wash through me. Sometimes I listen to the secret voice of the earth, of the earth's face being hollowed out and my fibrous fingers aching and muscle-bound. I feel like a tree, uprooting from my wife's sudden torturous ugliness. My wife wouldn't understand the kind of sacrifice I have made for my family. I didn't want to cheat her face out of its beauty and grace and magnificence, but I had a duty to protect my inner community. A wife who runs away? Someone has to take responsibility for her fugitive efforts. There are laws we men have to abide by. Fundamental laws about family and community. The role each individual has in the community of hands and mouths and legs. How would she feel if I ran away too? Wouldn't she have the right to cut my nose off too? Cutting my wife's ears off gave me power. It made me important in the community and it made me untouchable to other men. They saw how I was a model citizen! A man of my word. They saw how quickly I was willing to defend the law of the community and how much I was willing to sacrifice for it. Even sacrificing my wife for it. It has been long and true that a wife's beauty isn't important and should be hidden away like a song. I sing this song privately to my lips. In quiet, long hours where not a soul knows. I sing a sad song for the small river that lives inside of my manhood. It breathes, runs, and expands. My wife should know that I love her, unbridled, these effortless hours that march to and fro between other armies of hidden men.

THE ROOM IS BARE

THE ROOM IS BARE. A chair in one corner, dark. I see the particles in the air as I stomp back and forth, my callous, beefy hands behind my back. The day is crisp and I expect nothing more than to calculate my method. Be instrumental in my performance. I must be exact like an X-ACTO. No false step. No false step. Everything is in order. I study the room. A pile of shards shoulder their fragments against the foot of the chair. The room is flaking and smells green like algae. The shirtless man-boy has been shuffled into the room by one of my armed guards. He stands thin and tall like a birch tree with so many eyes inside him. His body can't see me but I can see him. I glance quickly at his nail-less fingers. His fingers are raw and infected. To amputate them is to be unreasonable. I have been told that I am a reasonable man. I act with great reason. I study his firm cheekbone. So angled like the corner of a metal table. I stare at his mediocre eyes. My assistant tells me that he is obstinate like an ox and no one has been able to pull anything out of him except his teeth. All his teeth except one. *WHAT DO WE NEED HIS FUCKING TEETH FOR? TELL ME WHAT WE NEED HIS FUCKING TEETH FOR?* We must remove his eyes. But first he must have breakfast. Breakfast is the most important meal of the day. My armed guard gives him another shuffle. I snicker; my mouth twitches. His footing is unstable and he collapses on the floor, a pile of puke near him. His breakfast. YES! YES! I had breakfast, a bit of spiced olives and a chunk of pita bread shuffled into my mouth. I am a horse. I am a horse. A horse. He is hunched over like a lizard. A scrap of notebook paper is stapled to his spotty hairy back. The handwritten scratches on the uneven paper identify him as 492. The staple cries two lines of dried blood. EAT! I yell. So he eats. I shuffle my legs back and forth.

THE EARTH NEEDS
A LITTLE MOUTH

I EYE HER FROM THE CORNER, my little girl. I eye her
a little each day, giving myself another look, another eye. I get
these ridiculous spells that make me think too clearly. I pinch my
fingers together, squeezing the tobacco inside the pouch before
shuffling it into my mouth. I sit here and I just sweat. I get so
bored staring at my girl. At the dumb field. Just dumb. I get so
angry I don't even understand why. Her hair is a mess, messier
than it should look. I could pour a bucket of dirt on her and she
would look cleaner. She is bent over, cutting the doll's hair with
a pair of rusted metal scissors. I have been thinking, looking at
the field and the sort, how the earth needs a little mouth. I have
an idea.

"Come here, cupcake!" I holler at her.

"But daddy, I'm busy playing."

"I SAID COME HERE!"

She walks over, her eyes still on her witch doll. I lift her chin so that her eyes are focused on me. They won't be going anywhere.

"You know what I want, cupcake?" I spit the tobacco onto the dirty carpet.

"No, daddy."

"I feel like cutting something."

"What do you want to cut?"

"I just feel like cutting something. Bring me your scissors."

"But I'm using it!"

"Bring me the FUCKING scissors!"

My little girl walks back to her doll. She never listens. I should just kick her instead of yelling at her. When did I get so soft? She lifts the scissors by the handle and it dangles like a metal rat by the tail in the humid air. But before she makes it completely toward me, I take it from her.

"Get on the table, cupcake!"

"Are we playing a game, daddy? What kind of game is it?"

"Well, it won't be any fun if you know what it is, right, cupcake?"

"Right."

She climbs on the chair and from the chair she climbs on top of the table. My little girl. Such a dumb girl.

"Lie down, Nat! Lie down!"

"Do I need to close my eyes?"

"If you want to."

When she lies down, completely down like her doll with its messy hair, I stare at her. The way she looks, so puffy. And her cheeks. I put the scissors right next to her leg. I walk toward the window and push the curtains apart.

"Daddy, that light is so hot!"

I walk up to her, tuck my hands beneath her buns and yank her yellow, floral underwear off her in one swift movement. It is like peeling a banana with two hands. I'd like to see what I can do with just one.

"You less hot now, cupcake?"

"Sure, daddy."

I lift her dress up and inspect her. It looks like a sleeping fortune cookie. What does she have in store there? It looks like the future needs some waking up.

"I am just going to see if you clean it clean enough. You don't want that part infected."

I spread her open with two fingers. I grab the scissors with my other hand. My girl jerks her legs up a little, her small buns tighten and convulse. I unclutch the scissors, its blades opening wide. I cut the tip of her small fleshy pearl. The sound that comes from her is like a human's.

A BRIEF ALPHABET
OF TORTURE

A)   CARVE OUT FIVE CIRCLES from the base of bare feet. Then insert five wine corks into these carved out ovoids. Ask the victim to walk like a geisha, one hand holding an orchid fan, the other hand brushing her lacquered hair back.

B)   Fasten the forehead and chin with clamps. Use two eyelash openers to crack the sufferer's eyes wide open. Pour hot boiling water onto the eyes.

C)   While the victim lies awake and fully conscious, begin removing the skin of the victim like deskinning a chicken. Begin first with the palm of the hand.

D)   I drag her by the hair, dragging her from one field
       to the next. Her body, a bundle of laundry, her hair,
       a black hemorrhage on my hands. I heave and drop.
       Heave and drop. I fuck her hard, my full penis a
       baseball bat, thrusting into her. Her nails digging
       like spikes into my arm, scratching me as if I itch.
       Her face and body undulate beneath me like the sea,
       turning blue with every thrust. My men are on third
       base with rifles, watching me as I overperform.
       Her nipples, two discs circling like hawks over CD
       drives. Later while I thrust, the men whip her hus-
       band's penis with their rifles like a drum. The mu-
       sic. Its incredulity. I am a muscular soldierly lizard
       on all fours, sprawling. My moon-shaped whitened
       buttocks, thick, pulsing, muscular. Her husband,
       chained to the fence, his eyes dropping like plucked
       feathers, wires poking through his skull, his with-
       ering, removed, startled gaze, his saliva spacious,
       his skin unsheltered, unfenced, and my anatomy at
       its full-blown consciousness, immune, permitting
       the susceptibility of her cunt. These impassable
       screams, blocked by one of my men who thrusts
       his baseball bat penis into her mouth. Her tongue
       blathering, bleeding, teething, teetering, balancing.
       It's all too soft, too Scottish, too much malt, too
       unschooled. It's simply this: the history of baseball
       bats—bats used to be made of ash but are now
       made of pine. When ash splinters as I splinter her,
       it runs through the pitcher's throat, as I run through

her. Her beginning. The dark clouds pulling each other by the nebulous hair, driven by the invisible hands of thunderstorms. She does whimper, does tatter, does atrophy a little, disappear a little into the faded timberland, the Acadian forest, soaking up her husband's irregular breathing, her heartbeat, ambient surround sound. When I am done pelvising her, pelleting her, she crawls away a little, a small whisper away, tattered piece of rag, her soft, buttermilk skin, her innocent blouse torn apart, the contrast, the bruises, the sharp definition of the blades of grass, and the sunrise, ambient and skylark, electronic textures, and calm again, not a single moan while rain comes rushing forth like horses. The hooves of the fluvial earth kiss precipitation like a child before a blue rose. It's done. Midstream.

E)   I enter her with my horsepower penis. A vehicle, transporting my blood into her blood. She eats cake a little by the windowsill while I pull all her hair out of her like pulling a horse out of a cow's vagina.

F)   It's defenseless, the rising sun of the desert. The peach, visible, defenseless, reveals the muted, satin, pale contours of her carved out nipple.

G)   I cut a child's smile out of her face like cutting heroin for a second dose of euphoria.

H) In the beginning, I open her like a rose, one petal at a time, with a razor blade.

I) Light, mild, and moderate.

J) Light, mild, and moderate.

K) Light, mild, and moderate.

L) Light, mild, and moderate.

M) I sprinkle salt on her butt cheeks before whipping her to death with a bamboo pole.

N) Light, mild, and moderate.

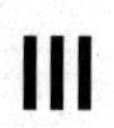

THE MYTH OF DARA CHROMOSOME

WHEN DUSK DESCENDS the charred topography, Dara has made it out of the countryside. She asks Timothy to wait in the courtyard for her. The gibbous moon makes a comma in the blue sentence of the sky while he walks gradually away from her, each step an adverb, deliberate. In a field of sunflowers, she removes her prosthetic limb, carries it up to her mouth, and blows vowels into its interior pipe. She calls to him, "Timothy! Timothy! Come here!" Timothy arrives leaving a pile of adverbs beneath his feet. He turns to her and whispers, "You are an imperfect being, Dara." Dara replies, "You left all of your adverbs behind. We might need them. But listen to the howling vowels of my imperfections!" Timothy pauses and replies, "Dara, if you toss them up and blow all your vowels in the sky, the moon will separate one imperfection from another." Dara wrinkles her nose and asks, "What for, Timothy?" Timothy takes the gibbous moon in his mouth and does not reply. But if he were to reply, he would say, "Because even imperfections need a moon or a pause."

ARRANGEMENTS

1.

HOWEVER STRANGE HER PENIS may look in the mirror, she has become accustomed to it. Like a guest that comes to her house first, uninvited, and second, unexpected. She thinks tea is a good idea. Serving tea with her protruding penis pressed to the glass of the stove. The penis hangs on her body like a dog's tongue hanging out of its mouth. At any moment, it might withdraw inside. But the guest doesn't have a cave to retreat and tea will be served very soon.

2.

She exuded an odor that I couldn't begin to elucidate or embody. I sat across from her and considered my options. The options seemed only limiting. I decided to wait on my decision. I waited too long, and the decision was made for me instead. Surprised and rather speechless, I watched her walk away. Her odor went with her. My jaw clenched. Terrified of what meaninglessness my life had just called forth in the absence of her odor. In the absence of her odor, I began to imagine my sorry life going downhill. Of course, life did not matter. In the instance the woman walked away, it began to matter to me. I watched the shadow of herself on myself run after her. My feet glued to the cement. As I watched her turn the corner, it dawned on me: the scent of her fleeing shadow and my nostril behaved like a man who had been in a coma for ten years.

3.

Retreating to her bedroom is not easy. There is a hairy man with a drawer around his arms. There has been an earthquake. In the midst of the quake, he flings himself onto the drawer and hasn't let go. He doesn't know where his life is located. He suspected that she is buried in the rubble with the two cats, Nylon and Import. The officials find Nylon on the street with a comb between her teeth and Import is standing around with a pile of crates where the forklifts huddle together like gigantic elephants. When the government comes to inspect the quake's damages, he does not let go of his drawer. The government and the officials attempt to persuade him to let go. They convince him that there are other drawers just like that in the city. Despite strong persuasions from important people from above, he clings onto the drawer like a second wife. When the night reaches near and the disappointed people leave for home, he releases the drawer and stretches himself across the crooked floor of the rubble. When he is finished stretching, he returns to the drawer and opens one of its slots. Inside, a seed the size of a pea begins to germinate. His children have grown like a plant inside of a pot.

THE WATERMELON BODY

THE MAN WAS NOT A WATERMELON, but the woman wasn't interested in his watermelon-less body. She insisted that he was a watermelon. She wanted him to be a watermelon. She wanted badly for him to be a watermelon. The more he thought about it, about desiring her and fulfilling her dream, the more he wished that he could reshape his body into a watermelon. He knew he didn't look anything like a watermelon. Unlike a watermelon, his exterior surface was pale and light and yellow. The watermelon's skin is predominantly verdant and has a camouflaged outer garment similar to an army uniform. The watermelon could be drafted into the war in the Middle East if it wanted to. His interior, on the other hand, was more like the interior of the watermelon: red and filled with seeds. Nowadays, they make seedless, genetically modified watermelons and when he asked her if she liked seedless watermelons, she shook her head so hard that he was scared that her neck would jackknife. Although there was a strong resemblance between the interior of the watermelon and the man, she recognized that his seeds were not dispersed equidistant from one another, as in the design of a perfect watermelon, but rather were located in one place in his body. She believed that sexually (there was no other way of looking at it), a watermelon was truly a perfectly designed man. Seeds dispersed throughout the body; his sexual belongings ubiquitously within reach. In other words, the woman found the body of a man with all the eggs in one basket as defective. Seeds should be scattered. If the watermelon man were to be attacked, he would not be vulnerable to infertility. Her logical conclusions about the male form, he found, were distasteful. He believed it took more courage to stash all the goods in one location. To separate the funds in different accounts was confusing, distressful, even dangerous, but, most importantly, it encouraged memory loss. It was impossible to keep track of all of them. She began to narrate to him about his watermelonness. She liked that he was bald, heavy, and was designed to explode. She liked that he was round and that a thick whisker floated out of his top like a muscular tail. She felt like he was an animal that, though unable to walk, could roll endlessly from one end of the world to the other. All he needed was a gentle push. She didn't mind being the apotheosis of that gentle push. She loved the simplicity of his watermelonness. There wasn't much to him: he could be cut into many pieces or left whole. His rind could be carved into watermelonesque architectures with unstable rooms and collapsible foundations. He would be carved into a flower. Basically, he could be anything she ever wanted him to be. She had always wanted to be with a black man. She knew that the watermelon was a black man and he had been born in Africa. She knew the watermelon loved public transportation. She knew this much about him and much more. She was appalled (her face dropped to the floor and could have dropped lower if it weren't for the floorboard) when he renounced his ancestry: the watermelonness and the blackness. Tell me, she asked him fervently and overwhelmingly, why are your seeds off-white when you were born in northern Africa? He didn't have an answer for her question. She asked a very good, noetic, and sound question. He didn't have any answers for her. He found that it was pointless to keep on denying himself before her. He didn't understand why he felt the need to validate what he was not. Perhaps he knew clearly and deeply (with conviction, if anyone else had asked him) what it was that he was not. He was more unclear about who he was. He began to think that it was the small-mindedness in him that encouraged him to weigh, to validate, to defend his position in society, and to alter her opinion about him. So what, he thought, if she thinks I am a watermelon. What was so outrageous about that? Yet it offended him. It made her happy and it did not negatively impact him socially or in the work force. She didn't work with him. She was just a neighbor who grew watermelons in her garden for competition and leisure. She kept on saying that her six feet by four feet plot was a plantation. She wanted to enter the Best Watermelon Competition in Delaware. She said that she was using him as a model for her watermelons. She found life and him unpredictable and exciting. He began to feel uncomfortable at an exponential rate around her. He thought that perhaps if he kept on confirming his watermelonness to her, she would want to have sex with him. Instead, she just wanted him there so that he could exemplify the empirical performance and appearance of a watermelon, one that sounded like a watermelon and looked like a watermelon. He was something that could easily be plucked out of her tongue. For her, delirious pleasure and nothing more. He decidedly decided that he should have sex with something like her kind. The more he thought about it, standing there, a fence between his gardenless garden and her plantation, the more he wanted to fuck her. She was on her knees now, pushing the head of one watermelon aside from the dirt. She had taken out a toothbrush and was brushing the dirt off the head of the watermelon. She ran the bristles along the smooth bald surface of it. She stroked it receptively and meditatively as if she were running a comb through a bald lamb. She worked slowly, taking careful care of the watermelon, as if she were taking care of a neonatal goddess. He wished that she would treat him the same way: slowly and with great tenderness. He desired her and her treatment of the watermelon very badly. He dashed to his car, drove to a grocery store 1.7 miles away, and returned home with a watermelon. He laid the watermelon on the kitchen floor, took out a knife from the drawer, and carved an inch off one end of the watermelon. He pulled down his pants and his boxers. He plunged in. It didn't have the suction quality he had experienced from a woman. In fact, it was sloppy, like getting a wet kiss from a messy mouth. It was terribly disappointing. He knew his penis had gotten sugary, though not on high-fructose corn syrup. He knew the shatterable architecture of the watermelon would collapse. He knew the content inside of it would relax and expand like blood vessels, but he felt deflated emotionally and physically. He got up, dripping, and wiped himself with a paper towel. He knew there was no point to life now. Then fear began to drive him into irrational thoughts. He got on a computer and googled about watermelon pregnancy. He had no idea if a watermelon was capable of getting big. He hadn't gotten hard. But he knew there were cases where a drip of sperm from a flaccid penis could still motivate gravidity. He certainly didn't want progeny from the thing he had partly carved and placed on the floor. He grew sad after googling about the uterus-less watermelon. At first, he feared having a son or a daughter and now he feared the opposite. He feared that he might never experience fatherhood. The neighbor didn't want to have sex with him. The neighbor believed that he was a watermelon. He remembered a fear once when he was eight years old. He had swallowed a grape seed. His mother told him that tomorrow a grape tree was going to grow in his stomach. She told him that drinking water would help nourish the grape tree into something big. He cried hard and didn't drink a drop of water. He tossed and turned in bed. When he felt pain, he thought it was the tree growing older and bigger. He didn't sleep a wink and was in a terrible state of mind. Now he had just had sex with a watermelon and the fear of the pregnant watermelon grew large in his head. Even though he googled about it. Even though the next day and the day after that the grape tree hadn't grown inside of him, an uncertain curtain of fuzziness in the sphere of reality prevented him from seeing what was true from what was untrue. He knew that a watermelon couldn't get pregnant, but, what if, he thought, this watermelon was capable of that. He picked up the watermelon and put in the freezer. He knew with certainty that nothing could grow from a frozen state. Everything stopped. Life stopped. Procreation stopped. If only birth control was as accessible as this, he would have solved population inflation and teen pregnancy. He would be a rich man and he could be anything and be with any woman he wanted. He closed the freezer door and sat down on the kitchen table. He tapped his fingers on the table and gazed outside. The neighbor was nowhere in sight. He had to go to work the following day. There was nothing else to do. He could sit here forever. He got up, walked into the shower stall, removed his clothes, and got under the shower head. His sugar-coated penis was stuck to his boxers. Too bad it wasn't a Post-it note. He would have loved to sit on the spine of a page and linger on the vast, immovable streams of words. He knew he would have a better life there. He knew that on a bookshelf, in a textbook, in a manual, in an important literary work, in a writer's reading selection, his penis would be the world's greatest placeholder. But he wasn't a Post-it note. He wasn't a makeshift anything. He felt he was just a perverted man in a shower stall, trying to rinse his procreation device of all the great possibilities of being a useful object in an objective universe. Tomorrow, he would be working on an assembly line of toothpaste tubes. He worked for Oral-B. They gave him free toothpastes and toothbrushes. He had given some of them to the neighbor as a sex-bribery device. The tactic didn't go very well at all. She had used the brush on the watermelon instead of her mouth. It had also been a gentle hint to her to brush her teeth more often. One time she leaned over the fence, her face so close to him that she was a blur, and whispered to him that she thought gardening was better than sex. Her breath stank. He remembered that the most. He thought that if he were to have sex with her, her mouth better smell right. She brushed the brush on the watermelon. Not only did the watermelon not have bad breath, it was completely hairless. He couldn't have been more appalled, bewildered and sad. He had grown wiser now. He knew that God didn't invent women to want him. God invented women to want watermelons and gardening. He knew that the power of giving things and making suggestions did not always correlate with the intentions of the giver. He knew there was much sacrifice in controlling what he couldn't control. He knew better now. He ran soap over his hairy chest and thought: too bad he wasn't a watermelon. But she had said that he was a watermelon. Suddenly he had a really good idea and couldn't wait to finish his shower to execute what he had in mind. He got dressed and walked over to the neighbor and rang the doorbell.

Silence.

And then, peeking out from the slightly ajar door, her nose. She opened wider. In her hand, she held a knife.

"Would you like a slice of watermelon? I am about to carve one," she asked him.

"Yes, please."

"Would you like to come in?"

"Yes, of course."

When he entered, she closed the door. When it was most

convenient for her, she stabbed him once on his back. Then twice. Then three times. Until he crumpled to the floor like a chair with one of the legs knocked out. And then, of course, he screamed. And then, she began to carve him. She carved him in the same way he carved his own watermelon. With one of his eyes still open, she asked him, "Would you like another slice of yourself?"

SEXUAL DOGS

SHE WAS A WOMAN who had acquired great wealth through hard work, though the public believed her prosperity came from inheritance. She did not suffer from childhood abuse and she was not one to endure emotional suffering due to negligence. In fact, as a child she had been very well loved, maybe even overly pampered, undoubtedly. She led a private life composed of disciplinary, solitary rituals. After a long day at work facing the skyscraper, she returned to her mansion with its view of skyscrapers, of minimal décor and intelligence, to eat a large bowl of iceberg lettuce sprinkled heavily with fried bacon prepared by her personal chef, Anton, a translucent glass of fine gin with ice, and a bowl of avocado sprinkled with nutmeg and salt. Her meal was elegant and always the same. After her meal, she gave Anton a stern, cold gaze, which forced him to scurry off her mansion floor like an unwanted cricket. She had developed a lust for undefined solitude, one which, over the years, was hard to keep up.

When they handcuffed her and led her down the long glass corridors of her mansion, and down one hundred floors via the elevator, the public and the paparazzi were quick to take snapshots. They were trying to capture the portrait of perversity. They discovered, quite to the contrary, that, based on the angle of her chin and the size of her stride, she was elegant to a perverse degree, and sophisticated, erudite, eremitic, and so loveable that their cameras became shy and apologetic and even ashamed to stretch their necks out for another snapshot. When she was handcuffed, she was wearing a knee-high skirt, black high heels, and a white long-sleeved blouse with ruffles unfurling down her chest, and when the police officers tucked her into the police car, it was like she was a handkerchief folded into a box. They were careful with her.

She had kept a personal sex service while she was single for many years. In fact, she had been single all her life. In the latter six years of her being before the incarceration, she became addicted to being licked. Though it wasn't an animal she had desired this from. She turned humans into dogs. Their sole job at her mansion was to become sexual dogs. She trained them carefully, with a few pre-organized and preordained gestures of her hands, to come and lick her. She underwent a thorough series of human acquisitions. She adopted and adhered to a clear code of hiring. Her rules were methodical and precise and almost random. She wanted women who were not too tall and did not talk too much and men who were not too scrawny or short and were muscular and blond, but not too muscular. She did not prefer academic men, but desired erudite women so that when the women licked her, they uttered educated moans that could only be murmured by a scholar in the midst of her deposition or thesis defense. And, most of all, she wanted her prostitutes to be virgin prostitutes; meaning, she was their first and probably only client.

Over the years, she developed an organized, consistent group of twelve rotating prostitutes who worked under her and for her. They had developed a syncopated schedule in which at least two men and two women were housed in her mansion at any given time. Whenever she felt an unpremeditated flash of delirious desire to be licked, and with the push of one red button from her remote control, one that looked like a remote detonator, the services of these men and women would deliver her unexpectedly-expected instantaneous and immediate high-quality sex service with their tongues to her clit. They arrived in a hurry, always naked, on all fours, panting social-cognitively and growling, to wherever she was located in the mansion—whether she was in her office writing emails to her subordinates or on her bed watching an episode of *Mad Men* or standing against her glass wall, watching the sunset disappear into the mouth of the earth.

She donned a silk robe. A prostitute came on all fours, bitingly and nippingly and slowly unraveled her underwear down her long legs, and if she were sitting on her netted, swivel gray chair, the prostitute would get on her knees and begin to dive slowly her tongue into her. She would lick the rims of her genitals in one full circle before beginning another slow circle. She preferred virgin prostitutes because often they did not know what they were doing and the untrained nature of their unjaded tongues gave her pleasure that she had came to call authentic and natural. She had learned through trial and error that professional and veteran prostitutes knew too well what they were doing and although she ultimately climaxed from their efficient work, she grew manically sad and unsatisfied. It took her six months to realize that the culprit of her lack of sexual satisfaction was the lack of freshness in the tongues amongst those she hired.

Sometimes she would stand leaning into the glass frame of her mansion. If she wanted the pleasure to be muscular and the texture of the tongue to be abrasive, a naked man, remotely commanded, would come on all four to pleasure her. He would open her robe slowly and without much provocation; he would spread her legs and begin to lick her while her naked butt rested against the glass.

Once, sitting in her room on a yacht on her way to Belize, the accompanying prostitutes came to her service frequently. She would be sitting by the window where the sea line and its waves were bobbing up and down. Sitting between sea and glass, with her hand holding a glass of gin and tonic and her legs spread wide open like the wingspan of a sea eagle, the prostitute gave her head. Her bobbing up and down matched the pattern in the sea waves. She realized that she loved being fucked, tonguewise, near the sea. There was something in the water, the sound of it or the silence of it, that syncopated emotionally with her clitoris. As if her clitoris could experience complex emotions such as regret and guilt without her. That her body was a glass bottle, the glass material, that separated itself from the liquid, which was her soul. That the vessel that gave her pleasure was driven by repetition and surface tension and from the surface tension, the undulating movement of the water, in which her entire being was being stirred.

Sometimes she wanted her prostitutes to lick her over the course of eight hours. Every ten minutes or so, they would dip their tongues into her, igniting her into a delirious state of hedonism. And as soon as her body regained her composure, her prostitute would circulate her tongue once again as if her clitoris were a library book on loan and had to be checked out and checked in again and again. The prostitute spent an entire day pleasuring her until her face cut open like light.

Sometimes she ran her fingers through their hair like they were the fresh grass of the earth. She combed their skulls meditatively, rhythmically, forgetting at times that they were still in between her legs, pleasuring her while her imagination went off on a hiatus. Sometimes she would be on the phone, making business calls abroad, but he would continue to lick her as if she had been sprawled out in bed waiting for the satisfaction to come. She kept these men and women in her house. They would become overwhelmingly bored at times, just waiting to lick her. And they would never know which of the four of them would come to her service. Slowly, they developed forced platonic relationships with each other. Under their legal contract with her, they were not allowed to fuck each other.

Although in each other's company they behaved like lonely and neglected dogs and cats whose owner had left them for long days of work or dining out, whenever they saw her, they were greedily excited to please her. She had a way of starving them emotionally and sexually. It was a way to guarantee the high quality of their services. When they saw her, they were truly genuine in their reception of her body into their lonely, aching mouths. Through emotional and physical starvation, they inadvertently became virgins. They were corporeally naked, but they were also emotionally naked. Most of her prostitutes all looked and acted the same over the years; they just simply became blurry faces and tongues. She had no emotional love for them. She treated them professionally and was generous with them financially. In fact, she paid them so well that they couldn't imagine leading a different life. They became addicted not only to her, but to the rich resources she provided them.

Outside of their six-figure salaries, she bestowed on them lavish gifts and vacations. And, through her own highly profitable company in the technology sector, she provided paid, premium health care to all the family and extended family members and friends of her prostitutes. Her health benefits were so extraordinary that if the prostitutes wanted an entire village under their health plans, she would provide it immediately and generously without asking questions. Over the years, the prostitutes, through

by shelves of thrift stores. Popped out on top of the left
he roof, he inserted a 2.75 foot titanium cylinder pump
g dishwasher soap which connected a plastic valve to
pump below the cabinet underneath the kitchen sink.
rains, Earl pulls a cord wired to the kitchen sink. The cyl-
mps out the dishwasher liquid in circular motions. The
s washed with apple-scent soap.

continuation with the House of Utensils, Earl ventures
unknown and laminates every inch of the siding, doors,
dows with forks. Beef forks, pudding forks, fish forks,
forks, tea forks, olive forks, chip forks, relish forks, cheese
aghetti forks, and dessert forks. He designs twelve of
lling's Venetian blinds with spaghetti forks. The spaghetti
ovelty, has metal shafts that hook to the end of the forks.
 or close all the blinds in the dwelling, the corpulent
 have to rotate or pivot a total of 2,400 spaghetti fork
arl implemented Spaghetti Fork Venetian Blinds into his
t originally as a weight-watching program to shed the
Orpha and he accumulated over twenty years. He regrets
sion. Either he proceeds with the Spaghetti Fork Vene-
ds to shed light naturally into the house, or he constructs
dows out of fish forks. They have no rotating devices or
d would permanently block the light from entering. The
 would become a titanium cave.

ion, he filled in the forks' lopsided & rectangular orific-
cherry oak and different types of dark and light wood
Santos mahogany, Australian cypress, Tiete rosewood,

the perversity of the capitalistic market, became slaves not only
to her, but also to their family or community.

But not all humans were designed to live over long periods of
time under her laws. Most were able to make the proper changes
to their life or lifestyles and stayed employed under her. But there
were those who simply couldn't take it. And these dogs, in fact,
one dog, led to her arrest. He had fallen deeply in love with her,
in fact. She had always known that love was the ultimate betrayal
and could foresee the betrayal unfolding under her aristocratic
nose. Under the contract, he could not legally sue her and did
not want to sue her. Under the terms of the contract, he had
agreed to be her dog. A loyal dog. He had agreed that he had
not been blackmailed into taking the position. He had signed the
lengthy 319-page document and under clause 145 section ii, he
could leave the position at any time his volition deemed fitting.
He simply possessed the natural tendency in its utmost unnatural
tendency to want her all to himself. In fact, he offered to provide
her, like a cellphone service, unlimited access to himself. At any
time and anywhere.

He promised that he wouldn't be burned out or face roaming
charges or go out of service. His love for her would defy the physical laws of the universe. He promised that her pleasure wouldn't
be compromised and that he had the natural ability to recalibrate
his virginity, providing her fresh sexual experiences each time.
But, in her unshakable logic, under the spell of his clear unrecip-
rocated love for her, she knew that even loyal dogs bite and are
fallible and have often bitten off the faces of innocent children.

She knew that his kind of love was one built on the reversal or imbalance of power. Under her mansion, he wanted to reinvent the rules. And, under the veneer of the extinct language of love, he had coined this power struggle "true love."

His dictatorship with love led her into the inevitable world of arrest. She was investigated and handcuffed. He managed to unionize all the prostitutes and convinced them that it was in-human and unethical for her to turn humans into dogs, sexual dogs. He convinced the court that she was a woman of inhuman perversity and that her existence was a threat to a stable modern civilization and while the economic world flourished under her leadership and entrepreneurship, the morality of man suffered greatly. The only way to protect the ethical providence of hu-manity was to quarantine her and convert her back into a human dog, a human-incarcerated dog. His inferiority complex was un-able to process and accept a woman in power, and through the propaganda of love, he attempted to dethrone her.

In prison, she was a sex figure with enormous prowess and au-thority. Under her rule, and always handcuffed, the inmates and security officers, all under her prison contract, were trained to lick her like virgin prostitutes. They even imported and served her iceberg lettuce, gin, avocado and nutmeg. And even salt.

THE HOUSE

TO ACQUIRE AND INQUIF

tells her to turn left at the three
and to turn north of the refrigera
named Earl and his wife, Orpha
and vendor, constructs a 1,120 ac
of utensils for his corpulent wife
garden east of their dwelling wher
dangle on clothes hangers.

Uxorious Earl delights his corpule
the entire roof welded out of ulu
kukris, hunting knives, bayonets,
knives, daggers, and knives he pu

the shab
end of t
containi
another
When it
inder pu
roof get

Later, ir
into the
and win
carving
forks, s
the dwe
fork, a r
To ope
couples
shafts. I
blueprir
pounds
the dec
tian Bli
the win
shafts a
dwellin

In add
es with
such a

Brazilian maple, knotty pine, Lyptus, African zebra, Sitka spruce, ziricote, Engelmann spruce, and Adirondack spruce. He welded the rest of the cracks with titanium. This prevented liquid from leaking into the dwelling. The Fork project took him two years to complete. His knife roof cut through the dark, dreadful hours of many storms. During those two years, his dwelling and over fifty thousand forks fought constantly with rain, snow, sleet, and wind. Through various sections of the dwelling, he thrusted three alcoves formed out of tar and over four dozen frypans for Orpha's reading pleasure. His genius overwhelmed her to the point where she couldn't decide which of the three alcoves she wished to throw her generous proportion over.

The flooring arrived last. Floored with spoons, spoons, spoons. Lined and mortified in symmetrical rows. Earl welded the entire flooring of the house with stainless steel bouillon spoons. The feat took him two years to complete.

Earl proceeded to wall the sections of his house with various utensils. For instance, his study room was walled with three different cutleries: forks, spoons, and knives. His wife's room was made entirely of spatulas and was a sanctuary where she made jewelry. Her neck was laced with forks, shaped spoon beads, and dully sparkled like a wind chime. She said the spatulas were like tiny squared mirrors. When thousands of them lined up in rows, she would be like a woman made of a thousand faces. She said she was not vain. He even said she was not vain. The neighbors even agreed she was not vain. But she was vain. Instead of making and producing jewelry like the way rats reproduce neonate rats, she spends her idle days staring at her reflection in the spatulas.

In the winter, they tell their guests to throw their coats on the fork stand hook.

One day, she is standing at their stove making feta cheese. He approaches her.

EARL: Orpha, come here, dear. I have a surprise for you.

ORPHA: What is it? What is it?

EARL: Sit on this sofa, please. Sit.

She sits. She sits and sits and sits.

He leaves and doesn't come back. Orpha falls asleep on the Russian sofa. Then, her husband shakes her shoulder.

EARL: Wake up, dear, wake up.

Her milk has gone bad. Very bad. He can't seem to decide with what material to wrap her gift he has made for her. He tries the cloth on the clothes hanger from outside, the hay in the byre, and towels from the bathroom. But none seems to fit.

She sits up. Awake and alarmed. He hands her the spatula box. He says, open it. He is on his knees between her legs. She spread them apart for him. Open it. Inside is a glittering thing. The most luminary thing she has seen since he surprised her with the spatula room. Inside is a purse made of hammered spoons.

She opens the clasp and looks suspiciously inside. Inside is a tiny apricot.

EARL: So what do you think?

ORPHA: Very tonic, dear. Very tonic.

She dashes off immediately to her room. Her spatulatic room. Closes the door. Eats the tiny apricot silently to the core. When she is done, she puts her jewelry away. She puts some of her necklaces in her purse along with the apricot seed. She walks out of the room. Her husband has fallen asleep in the same manner in which she had fallen asleep when he was waiting for her at the apricot tree. Waiting for her response to his proposal. His shoulder slants to the right, and his legs spread moderately apart.

His legs speak:

Wild day for a wild man on the run. Running from the oven and refrigerator. Running with his heart in a sugar canister. And with wild madness, he begs and begs and begins to run again. His canister bouncing against his chest. The glorious sun dances around his body. The heat and secretion fall off his body. But he runs. His wife's heart is in a canister. Coated in sugar. Hopping up and down like a girl on trampoline inside some dark vault. Everyday she hits the surface or comes to the surface. Her mouth finds her first, then her nostrils, and then her ribs. Later in the night, her upper torso slides across the table, juxtaposed against the skin of the heat. Each gesture takes her away from him. In the deep valleys, hidden and forlorn, dank hours where the sun arches its black back across the mulberry trees, across the lake, and across the aching body of a cow moving slowly through the field. Life feels good. Sweat feels good. And so she is born. He is born. Like a machine into the organic and then into mechanical age. Their hearts and organs ushered like pickled apricots and cucumbers into titanium canisters.

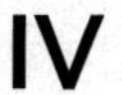

I ASK THE SENTENCE

I ASK THE SENTENCE to move across the carpet floor.

I ask it to not drag its paragraphical legs while doing so.

I ask it not to be lonely, not to have ethical issues with women with menstrual cramps, or periods, and whatnot.

I ask the sentence to conduct itself in a way that does not deny the social conditions of other sentences, that does not make any sentence feel left out or suicidal.

I ask the sentence to be chivalrous, to open semantic doors for women, and not to treat children as linguistic concubines for imperial expansion.

I ask the sentence not to open fire on any other sentence.

I ask the sentence to be self-reliant, to use itself as a mirror for narcissistic reasons and not to ask other sentences for monetary support.

I ask the sentence not to hypnotize other sentences, so that they don't become organ donors to objects, nouns, pronouns, and indirect objects.

I ask the sentence not to be an alcoholic, not to inebriate streams of consciousness, the passive voice, C. D. Wright.

I ask the sentence to be reasonable in a Haitian ransom, just five more sentences, just five more sentences and I will let your mother, the paragraph, go.

I ask the sentence not to leave her semicolon inside a hot van in the middle of the summer and to leave the Budapest train station, but never to walk 105 miles to the border of Austria.

I ask the sentence not to write that sentence; you know that sentence, the one where it has too much hypermasculinity in it, the one with the toilet lid up, you know that one.

I ask the sentence to please, to please marry Gary Lutz.

FURTIVE BRAS

THE BOOK ARRIVES SO SLYLY, so furtively. As if the bell around its neck has broken, muffled by the tissue. The noise and emptiness of the hallway. It climbs a flight of stairs with its wings embalmed, swallowing in its darkness.

Words flying, swimming, twirling in the body of their text.

Pages diving into each other's depth: a book unopened, climbing a flight of stairs.

She is awake. Light flutters through the curtain, hangs on the wall, slivers down its whiteness. Outside: brass, wind, percussion. The marching band marches, drumming on the taut

membranes of their sparkling instruments. Stretching. Re-flex-
ing. The mellifluous sound quivering in her ears. She thinks this
is soothing.

For seven days, she watches bras and marching bands come and
not go. The FedEx man says, sign here please. She signs beside
the X, closing the door. Closing quietly.

She lies supine on the large king bed thinking about the bras
from Canada. They have stripes around their petite cups. Who
would have known that beneath their elegant exterior a tiger har-
bors its appetite?

From the corner of her eyes, she watches the woman try them
on. The tiger admires himself in the mirror. He multiplies two-
fold, standing in front of the reflective glass. The tiger opens his
mouth but does not roar. The woman turns sideways. She has a
look, as if her bra—a tongue, dancing, undulating on the body
of the mirror. Gazing at herself makes her heart throb.

Alice has awoken from a fragile dream. The marching band
screams her alive. She wakes up believing she is contained. She
wakes up believing life owes her everything. The apartment, the
bookshelves, the orchid, the sandals, the hanger, the toothbrush,
the photo frames, the spatula, nail polish, the stapler, the dish,
the sweater, the CD player, the watch, the pen, the ocean, the
universe, the galaxy.

The book opens itself upon her touch. It has arrived slyly, furtively. UPS and FedEx men do not behave the same in their delivery. She likes the one who leaves a package leaning against the door and quietly walks away. He does not leave a trace of his existence or presence. Books and bras are not delivered—but arrive on their own terms, of their own volition.

The UPS man is the universe. He arrives at her door like a stygian script.

The FedEx man is man's reasoning on existence. He needs a signature to validate his arrival.

She watches the woman throw on a shirt of ecru. The tiger roars. No one hears him. The woman walks away from the mirror as she uncurls the gossamer hem of the shirt to cover her belly. The book dangling on the edge of the bed. She reads a line. It says:

She said butter was colored with marigolds.

Her head falls on the fluffy pillow, and she sighs. Having no clue what it means, she sighs again. She watches light dancing on the wall and wonders at what time of day the moon draws the sun into her bosom. When does she undress his yellow toga and bathe him in her voluminous darkness? She desires that time of day. The frankness. The nudity of a moment. She desires those too.

On the page, each word is spaced from another word. It holds on the page, all the solitude the world can muster. In her reading, the words climb onto each other. A snake on sand. A man on a woman. Light on a wall.

The climbing of words, and a solitary thought emerges. Reading is an art. It has to be. How then can aesthetics be appreciated?

She crawls out of bed. The cloistered thought tosses itself on the walls of her mind. As she stands up to collect and spread it out to make sense of it—the sentence that hangs off the edge of her hippocampus—it shatters into stars. With all the concentration it takes, she reaches out into the darkness of her mind's universe. All of the stars pinned to the sky, not a single one resembling that singular thought.

Is it butter?

Flying marigolds.

Reassembling the words. Alice feels hopeless. And then impotent. She doesn't want to resort to the book as the sole means of reasserting concreteness. That one absconding, eluding, slippery sentence. Butter climbing on marigolds. Or was it marigolds climbing on butter? The sentence makes her die a bit. In her anguish, she reopens the book. Flipping the pages. Flipping. Scanning. Scanning. Flipping. Scanning.

Where is it?

Shuffling amongst the mass of other words. Butter falling off marigolds.

There it is.

She said butter was colored with marigolds.

The book falls down onto the pillow. Closing its 96-page eyes and sleeping quite soundly, quite softly, quite tenderly. Something was done to butter in the garden of language. Something egregiously magnificent.

Marigolds.

The sound of the marching band drums through the windows and walls of her apartment as she turns the knob. Water begins to fill the tub. Alice peels open the plastic curtain, climbs in, and lifts the nozzle. The coldness of the water flows down her body. She is naked and her toenails have a thick layer the color of dark maroon. She feels more naked with ten maroon nails doused under a thin coat of water.

She thinks dark maroon is the color of a slut. This slut walks out of the shower with a towel wrapped around her chest. This slut considers her options; makes a to-do list.

Water the orchid.

Take the trash out to the large, communal dumpster.

Re-shelve the books.

Bake banana bread for the fundraiser.

Make the bed.

Leave seller feedback on Amazon.

This seller is troublesome. The book arrives without a single scratch on its head. It arrives through the door very slyly, furtively, unlike the bras from Canada. Excellent choice of postal service. Excellent seller. Would purchase from this seller again.

Out of the shower, she notices the woman with roaring bras sitting on the bedroom windowsill smoking a cigarette. Looking pensive and meditative. One exhalation. Two exhalations. Ephemeral rings ascend the crepuscular stairs. The woman is spending her afternoon puncturing holes on the thin sheet of atmosphere. The woman thinks the sky can't breathe without the holes for ventilation, or perhaps she thinks the rings are perfect conduits for stranded ghosts to re-enter other worlds. She is the ancillary servant of Charon. He carries coins across the Styx and Acheron. She is a sympathizer for those on whom Charon does not bestow coins. She blows rings out of her scarlet lips for those left behind.

She watches the woman on the windowsill as she straightens the cover over the colossal bed.

Marigolds fall out of the eyes of the book. Like rain. Like tears.

The book opens on the palm of her hand. She thinks of the desiccated orchid drugged in dark soil. The book opens and opens on the palm of her hand. She wonders if she can water the plant from her mind's eyes. Will the orchid notice the difference?

She grabs the pitcher, pours the liquid into the pot. This is only a vision from her mind. Yet, it's quite a task for her imagination. She realizes that there is a great deal of cleansing in the corporeal act of performing a task. A lightness. Quite porous. Quite easily fitted into the scheme of her menial chores. Conceptually, an onerous heaviness that sags her spirit down. In the future, she will water the plant and think very little of it in the process.

The woman at the window exhales the last drag of her cigarette. She flicks the butt out of the window. Alice contemplates, Why do women buy beautiful bras, tiger-striped, and not a soul can hear them roar, or sing in colors like butter dyed with marigolds?

No one could view them, really. Their sexy, lacy allure. Not the mailman, not her non-existent lover, not the landlord, not the neighbors.

Must sexiness stay indoors?

Beneath a thin veil of fabric?

When the bed is made, she crouches in a corner. A towel still wraps itself around her bodice. She notices light emanates through the closed blind of the window in the hallway. The small white fingers of the little sun peeking through. A few drops of light bubble on the wooden floor. Five ivory buttons created by the imperfection of the blind's design. Five buttons dancing naked in the darkness of the hallway. From the ceiling's view, the hallway looks like a sleeveless shirt.

Alice crawls on the hard floor and lies on her back. She closes her eyes. The coolness of it. In phrasing a moment. In phrasing a moment, she listens to the drumming of her heartbeat. She gains consciousness. She loses consciousness. Her head becomes light. Nothing. Then it becomes heavy. Everything. She begins to have a lucid dream. A woman in black miniskirt, shirtless, wearing a black bra talks to her. Could you lend me a button? She asks. Alice, feeling rather muted, shakes her head. Please, she begs, I have an interview. The woman grabs her nipple, mistaking it for a button. She grips the black blouse on the bed and presses it to Alice's chest. She pins her to the wall. She struggles a bit, before popping Alice's nipple through one of her blouse's slits. Alice looks down. Her mind makes a silent scream. The color doesn't match, she tells her. And Alice slaps her hand. Please, she begs. I have an interview.

Alice flickers her eyes open. Her eyes drink in the room's hazy composition. A blur. She peels off the tucked corner of the towel. The first flap falls softly on the floor and then the second flap. Slowly she walks her right hand over her nipples to make sure they are still there. Her fingertips tinge the nipples like Braille, reading her breasts—a haiku script. They confidently confirm her state of consciousness. Though she is completely naked, lying on the wooden floor.

Taking her time savoring the last tang of the nicotine, the woman at the windowsill has ceased staring out at the happenings beyond the window and has shifted her attention to the woman on the floor.

Her eyes travel first on Alice's nipples, down the black triangle, and the article that heightens her attention the most—the ten painted toenails. The ten maroon dots, like buttons, dance on her alabaster toes. Vestal. Rare. Seductive toes. She becomes aroused. She cannot determine the source of her desire. Is it the nicotine? Or the painted toenails?

Alice, she says softly, you look like a fallen angel. Where are your bras?

They are underneath the wooden floor. Absconding. They are beneath my toenails. Absconding. Do you hear them roar? These furtive bras.

She presses her ear on the wooden floor and listens to the sound of trees, timber, the corridor of desire. The ear of the wood listens back. The skin of the labia. Its intricate, woody lips. Palpitating on her ear. The woman watches her. Alice gets up, leaving the crumbled towel where it is, and climbs onto the made bed. She opens the book and reads a line from it.

Stroke my loins.

She closes the book. Lets it fall onto the pillow. This afternoon Alice is planning on painting the woman's toenails.

One stroke at a time.

One stroke at a time.

WINTER ROSE

WHEN IT RAINS, WHICH IT HASN'T. At least not lately. But when it rains, which can be in the spring or fall, Nicole's nipples become alert and her vulva swells up with clouds of feelings and illusions. It's winter now, yet her nipples continue to move in the same state of awareness, a type of visceral consciousness in itself that is impervious to the concrete world, at least it would like to think so. This morning, standing like an obscure fixture on the ceramic kitchen floor, she observes the exterior world, looking out the window above the large, oval kitchen counter, where lies the earth's floor expanding its barren bleakness into the heart of the horizon. She returns to the dining table to continue her breakfast. The pair of eggs stares back at her admiringly.

Out of the corner of her eye she notices several fanned-out blotches of crimson-painted petals on the ceramic floor. Before she can get up to search for a rag to wipe them away, her lover quietly slips herself into the adjacent seat and begins to pour a rain of flakes into her bowl. The sound emits the cracking of five hundred autumn leaves on a burning afternoon. Right in front of her eyes, an opaque vase glows at the center of the table with a rose wedged inside it. She can't help but realize, in that moment, that the solitary rose looks and behaves like a crimson penis. Several days ago, it appeared like a strawberry muffin top. When time ages it, this penis blooms and continues to bloom. Each petal crumbles onto the table, dried and sterile and shriveled—and lost.

"Sage," she asks, "Why would someone present a rose to symbolize eternal love? A rose *is* the apotheosis of ephemeral representation. It lasts only days. At most, a week."

"I don't know, dear," is her soft, vacuous reply. Sage reaches over to part her lover's hair to one side. She likes the way Nicole's face is shaped, oval and straight. Sage's long fingers, like stems, linger on her soft cheek.

Nicole wonders whether, if the red rose inhabited a different place, say a wet, moist, damp place—would it thrive and become more itself? Or would it become waste and decompose before it enters the life of blossoming? Good thing it was only one rose. She doesn't really know if she could handle a dozen. Later, while cleaning up the table after breakfast, much later in the evening, when the sun emanates a soft glow and vanishes, she picks up a few petals and places them in the trash bag. Essence of the male member in a black, smelly void. It will spend the rest of its life withering slowly, awfully, and perhaps with a type of moisture no one wants to know, or smell. The rose in the tall vase still stands. Stands erect with its head nodding to one side, acknowledging the knowledge it knows very little about.

Sage urgently leaves the table and enters the bathroom down the hall, leaving her lover to contemplate the rose. From the bathroom's diminutive window, Sage can see the misty hands of cold dew climbing quietly on the window's quartered veins. Each climb is evaporation. Each climb is an obliteration of reality. Each climb is ascension into the unknown. Today, although no longer itchy in un-scratchable places, she is still very aroused— aroused by the daylight that beams out of her nipples, radiating like antennae. Before the rose, she had thought about nothing but her breasts this morning. They are alive, their eyes alert and watching the world behind a beige veil which is their only current window. Her uterus is moist with desire and the rest of her corporeal expressions are dense with titillation. Outside, a few weeks before winter hit quite suddenly, a squirrel perched like a bird on top of a tree. When it climbed down with its head towards the ground, she remembered thinking how well the squirrel blended and camouflaged itself with nature, how for a split second it felt as if the tree were climbing itself. Winter has stripped the tree of its protective garment, leafless and completely de-robed with its no-longer-green hair tangled and suspended above the ground, and no longer demented as it was last summer.

She asks, "Tree, why do you bathe naked in winter's lagoon?"

She is sitting, bottom parallel but legs vertical to the floor. Each month her body builds a home. And each month when no one decides to live in it, her body learns to demolish it. The blood must drip. It's dripping. It's dripping because the moon is collaborating with her uterus. It's coming. And she watches it through a narrowed window, a rose blooming out of a narrowed wall, through the reticent lips of her gender's voiceless voice. Roses for her bathroom's vase. Roses for a non-child that must enter from one world into another. Shivers and chills run down her spine.

If love can't be seen through the symbolism of a rose, through what can it be seen? Can it be seen through the dank window of her toilet bowl?

She imagines the rose still. By the end of the week, more petals would have fallen onto the table and scattered on the floor. Some of them will curl up, and some will languish on the wood surface. Perhaps the penis is losing itself to time and gravity. The petals on top of its head will be pruned. The rose would look pruned. Extending her mind's finger, Nicole touches its center. So soft that it is like touching nothing. The penetrator keeps on penetrating—onto a threshold of ennui. She has never been with a man who has deflowered himself for her, who opened and continued to open in his opening. So, naturally, optically experiencing this rose in its deflowered state is a virginal experience She must be the homosexual man, entering the man, the he-rose, and finding himself vibrating and quivering. But can this be love, the syncopated meeting of two different heads, both gliding on each other's soft and hard flesh? Could this be love, the tree climbing the tree?

Nicole knocks, and opens the door as Sage wipes the blotches of roses away. Her head peeks in, hands covered with broken egg shells, feet as rooted as ginger, and she asks, "Do you want a jar to nurture the menstrual content?" She tells her, "No, not this month." This month, the roses emerge in liquid. If they had delivered themselves in solid form, perhaps quasi gel-like, they would have had a place at the kitchen's window. So the moon could have something of itself to look at during those grave one hundred autumn days.

Sage reenters the kitchen. She finds Nicole on her knees on the ceramic tiles in the midst of washing the red blotches with a wet white cloth. An aluminum bucket three-quarters full of water situates itself near her right arm.

"Let it be," Sage tells her. Her smile spreads across her face. The smile, wicked with elation, opening like the breaking of sacred bread.

She bends down; her thick beige dress opens like a Japanese fan on the ceramic floor. She bends down and delivers a kiss to her lover, whose eyes are illuminated with passion. She leans over to collapse into her arms, the way the wind bends its will against the stalwart tree. In leaning, in collapsing, she kicks the bucket and the water spills, flooding the ceramic floor. They both break into giggles. The room echoes, bouncing the ebullient noise against the white walls. And then they become serious, their lips smooth out the lines, the skin around their eyes loses its grip, and they become lost, trapped, inside the windows.

The windows of each other's eyes. The windows of each other's bodies. When the house was built, it must not have been symmetrical. It must have been lopsided. It's actually slightly slanted. Water flows to one side, collecting in the far corner before bouncing like demented balls down the stairs. The water splashes and drips, bouncing and dripping. She holds Sage's gaze before her body takes over.

When she elevates her pelvis

When she elevates her pelvis for a kiss

When she elevates her pelvis to meet Sage's, their lips seal a kiss.

When she lifts the dress over her lover's body. And when they climb on to each other like a tree climbing a tree. When she is denuded, ripping open her lover's blouse. When she is not with child. When two windows face one another on a bleak winter day. When water soaks open the doors of their bodies. When in the bleak winter day, when she elevates her lover's pelvis to converse, lips to lips, breath to breath. When four windows greet each other on a bleak winter day.

The furnace rumbles. And the refrigerator sizzles. Outside, the cold is sneaking in. Inside, the warmth is exuding out. When her doused body is pinned against the old, wet kitchen tile, the color of white pearl, four breasts, four cups cupping each other, four cups of Rioja clinking in a toast. This is a toast. The lovers are feasting on each other's bodies, feasting. Window to window. Lip to lip. Pelvis to pelvis.

And when four windows view each other on a bright Monday morning, the whitest of lights illuminates through all the other's windows. The exchange of different cups of love. She is spread out. She spreads her out like an accordion. In reflex, she folds back in, and in deflection, she is spread out. Again. When her fingers, like stems, intertwine and grip the other body in the ride. When two currents of liquid rose collaborate, merge, sharing the same currency.

When lights radiate during that time of month, on a bleak winter day. When two bodies climb each other, riding each other, riding into the dank window of the void.

When the floor is empty of water. When part of the floor is wet and moist, and the other part dry. The lovers ride, kiss, carve each other's bodies until they have become solid clay. Two halves wedge together to become a ceramic vase. Out of that orifice two red ribbons emerge, interlacing, stitching the eye of each body, its red current, and a rose sprouts out of the ceramic floor.

V

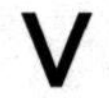

THE BOY
AND THE MOUNTAIN

[MY FATHER AND I ARE ASCENDING the mountain together. He says that my thirteenth birthday is today. It is a day to celebrate my birthday and to celebrate my father's death. Today is the day to talk to the mountain. My father dreams of bending and falling at the top of the mountain. We are going very slowly. We start at the base. One foot after another. We have started very early. We were up before the sun was up. I do not want to relinquish myself to the mountain, but my father insists that we must. My father plans to lean into the side of the mountain and pass away. This is what he tells me before we leave the house. He is going to whisper the pages of his gene pool into death and onto the mountain. I must be willing to consider this. This is his dream. This is the reason why we are climbing the mountain.]

FATHER: We must stroke the back of the mountain with our footfalls. The mountain lives on rain, on sun, on thunderstorms, on snow, but also on the sweat of our footsteps. How will she know that she has not been forgotten by the humans?

[To talk to the mountain from her top is just as important as to talk to the mountain at her foot. When we were at the foot of the mountain, it was still dark, and light had not collected dusk around our feet. At the foot of the mountain, my father gets on his knees. He bends his head and asks me to get on my knees and bend my head. I go on my knees and lower my head. He begins to talk to the mountain as if it were his mother.]

FATHER: Mother, we must climb up you. My son and I are requesting permission to climb up you.

[Silence from Mother Mountain.]

FATHER: I know you have been unresponsive. I have taken your silence as approval.

[Silence from Mother Mountain.]

FATHER: Please show us signs if you disapprove.

[Silence from Mother Mountain.]

FATHER: We must climb, son. There is plenty of time, but we
must move as if we have no time.

BOY: Okay, father.

[We climb breathtakingly fast. Father says that he knows the way
to our destination. He says 'up.' But I do not think father knows
what he is talking about or he may, in fact, not know the way. We
have not been climbing up as he declared. We have been moving
along the side of the mountain, almost sideways. This is not up.]

BOY: Father, I do not think we are moving up.

FATHER: We are, son.

BOY: If we are moving up, why does it feel like we are moving
sideways, father?

FATHER: In order to move up, we must go sideways.

BOY: Okay, father. If you think so, it must be so.

FATHER: It is so.

[We continue to climb. I carry a light neon-colored backpack.
My father carries a heavier red backpack. My father walks slower
steps. He uses his wooden canes for balance. I use my canes to
understand my fear. The mountain is hard. Each time my flexible
canes land on the hard rocky surface of the mountain, I begin
to think that life is very short and it could break at any moment.
The landing of my canes is a reminder that my breath may no
longer be my breath. And, if I long for something, I must long
for it now before it is too late. I ask father about his dream.]

FATHER: It just came to me.

BOY: How did it come to you, father?

FATHER: It just did.

BOY: Will it come to me, father?

FATHER: I do not know.

BOY: This is your dream.

FATHER: This is my dream.

BOY: Father, how far must we push the body of this dream?

FATHER: I do not know, son. But we must continue.

BOY: How far into the future must we go, father?

FATHER: Not very far, but far enough.

BOY: Father, when will we rest?

FATHER: Soon.

[We climb for a very long time. We do not speak. I do not know why we do not speak, but we do not. I have stopped questioning everything. I begin to believe that if I talk I may lose my oxygen capacity. I do not want to be more breathless than I have to be. Climbing is an indirect way of giving away my life. Each breath counts. Each breath will surrender itself to the mountain. But when my father speaks, I must speak. I will certainly give away a few breaths for my father. He is my father, after all.]

FATHER: One day this dream will be your dream too.

BOY: I do not think so, father. This dream won't be my dream.

FATHER: What will you do?

BOY: I do not know, father. I simply do not know.

FATHER: You are thirteen now.

BOY: Yes, I am thirteen.

[We stop to take our water canteens from our backpack. My father retrieves his from the backpack first. He offers it to me first so that I do not have to take mine out. I take small sips and then bigger sips. I hand the large canteen over to my father. He takes big sips and then bigger sips. My father's load will get lighter because of our hunger for water, as if we share the same strands of understanding.]

FATHER: My load will be lighter now.

BOY: Certainly, father.

FATHER: We did not drink from your canteen. We did not drink from your canteen because it is harder to go from a rich state to a pauper state.

BOY: Yes, father.

FATHER: You must learn not to relieve weight or add more weight to your body than you have to. The weight on your back must maintain a status quo.

BOY: Why, father?

FATHER: Any change will lead to grief. I do not want your body
to grieve.

BOY: Even if it is a good grief, like a lighter load, father?

FATHER: That's not a real grief. It is a deceiving grief.

BOY: Why is that so, father?

FATHER: When your body is used to a particular weight, it has
attained a particular comfort level with itself. And
then its comfort state will snowball into a greater
comfort. At this state, you will not want to climb up
any more, but you will be motivated by your body to
climb down. This is a dangerous place to be.

BOY: Father, this is very dangerous for you indeed. We have
drunk a lot of your water. What will you do?

FATHER: I will add a few rocks to my backpack. The rock must
carry as much weight as the water we just drank.

BOY: This is a very difficult mathematical problem, father.

FATHER: You were wondering how we were able to measure
this. I have the perfect solution, son. I brought us a
digital scale.

BOY: But, father, didn't you say to climb the mountain we must
only bring the survival essentials?

FATHER: I certainly did say that.

BOY: But a scale is not an essential, father. It cannot feed, warm, or heal us.

FATHER: You were merely thinking of the physical wellness, son. I was watching out for our emotional fitness. A scale is a symbol of balance. I have brought the most important tool for our survival.

BOY: I see, father. Shall we find rocks now for you and for me? For your emotional wellness and mine?

FATHER: Of course. How much did you drink from the canteen, son?

BOY: I drank a few small sips and a few big sips.

FATHER: How many ounces were those?

BOY: I do not know. How can we weigh that which has escaped into my throat and your throat, father?

FATHER: My throat does not matter. I do not have to substitute rock for water because the weight has redistributed in my body. We must calculate the weight of water that you have slipped into your mouth.

BOY: Father, how can we begin to do that?

FATHER: I do not know, son. We must not move on until we figure this out.

BOY: Had I drank from my canteen, we would not have this problem to begin with.

FATHER: You must not think this way, son. You must not re-
cede into the past to retrieve a solution to your current
problem. You must look forward.

BOY: Yes, father. What must we do?

FATHER: Let us sit on the edge of this cliff and think.

[Father and I sit down on the edge. My head is blank. What is
inside of my father's head is unclear to me. I do not have access
to his thinking. I imagine it is as blank as mine is. And if it is as
blank as mine is, we must not be thinking. And if we are not
thinking, we are doomed to this edge till eternity. I begin to cry.]

FATHER: Why are you crying?

BOY: I am crying because my head is blank and we are doomed,
father.

FATHER: We must not get ahead of ourselves.

BOY: You said to look forward for a solution. I have gazed forward, father. And all I see is hopelessness.

FATHER: You have looked too far, son. Far enough so you can
move, but not so far that you are unmovable.

BOY: But how far is too far?

FATHER: When all you see is hopelessness, it is going too far.

BOY: I see now, father. What distance does blankness cover?

FATHER: What do you mean?

BOY: All my mind sees is blankness. Is that going too far?

FATHER: It is going at a perfectly good rate.

BOY: Are you sure, father?

FATHER: I am not too terribly certain. But I am pretty certain.

BOY: How far is blankness, father?

FATHER: Not very far at all. In fact, its farness is moving at the same rate as our sitting down is moving.

BOY: Really, father?

FATHER: Really, son.

[My father and I sit together in silence and in blankness. I have no clue as to how to help my father. My father's state of mind is completely blank and he is hardly being despondent about it. I allow my thoughts to quiet down. I gaze up at my father. The sun has not climbed over the earth. Thus, I sit in the darkness with my father. The sun must be sitting at the bottom of the earth waiting just like us for an opportunity to climb up. Sitting in the darkness with my father has taught me several things. The silence is hypnotic and mesmerizing. I do not hear my footsteps in the dark as I had earlier. If my father were sweating, I would not know it either.]

BOY: Father, have you been sweating?

FATHER: I do not believe I have.

BOY: We must not have climbed very hard then, father.

FATHER: Why did you ask?

BOY: Must we not calculate the weight of our sweat as well? We must not permit our grief to get away from us.

FATHER: You are wise, son. It has not occurred to me to take our sweating into consideration. We must calculate your water intake, how much I sweat and you sweat, and how much water to retrieve from your canteen, and then we determine how many grams of stones we must insert into my backpack.

BOY: This is a lot to calculate, father.

FATHER: I feel slightly despondent, son.

BOY: You do not know where to go from here, father?

FATHER: I do not know what to do.

BOY: I do not know what to do either, father.

[We sit in silence, my father and I. I believe we are doomed. If we do not come up with a solution, we must abandon my father's theoretical mindset. But I do not think he is ready to let go of that. He is deeply attached to his thinking. I do not want father and I to die out here. I do not want anybody to die out here because of a theoretical framework. I think life is higher than any logical construct.]

BOY: Father, when can we abandon your theory on balance?

FATHER: Why are you so fast and so ready to quit, son?

BOY: I do not think we have hope, father.

FATHER: I have brought enough for the both of us to survive on.

BOY: You said you were despondent earlier, father.

FATHER: I did say that, but stating how I feel at a particular moment in time does not dictate how I feel in the long run.

BOY: Must we wait here forever, father?

FATHER: Why are you so anxious to get going? Do you find the company of the dark intolerable?

BOY: A little, father. Darkness with footsteps does not feel like darkness at all.

FATHER: Just because you are moving doesn't mean that you are impervious to fear, son.

BOY: I know, father. I just miss the companionship of footsteps, that is all.

FATHER: We have been talking. Talking feels like the fall of footsteps, not necessarily with our feet, but with our mouth. How can you say you miss the companionship of footsteps when they have not left you at all? If we are in complete silence for a little longer, perhaps I can begin to understand your nostalgia for footfalls. But we have been very noisy. We must allow our existence to carve silence into this mountain for a little longer so that we can miss them. When we miss them, then we have made better companionship for our footfalls as we have become a little more appreciative of them in their absence.

BOY: I do not understand your logic, father. It feels wayward.

FATHER: In what ways is it wayward?

BOY: In all ways, father. I can still miss things even if they have not departed from me. And duration does not always dictate nostalgia. There is no time gauge or constraint in that. The absence of light does not indicate darkness. The absence of light is what it is, father, the absence of light.

FATHER: The absence of light does indicate darkness. We are in the dark because there is no light.

BOY: I do not understand, father.

FATHER: What do not you understand, son?

BOY: The logic of that does not fit in the fabric of my reality.

FATHER: The logic states that we are in the dark because there is no light.

BOY: Yes, father. We are in the dark, but not because there is no light. We are in the dark because light has not come yet. Light is still here. It just goes somewhere else first, or darkness has covered the skin of light. Light and darkness exist simultaneously, father.

FATHER: I can see some truth in that.

BOY: Yes, father. Perhaps we must learn to clothe the skin of darkness to see the naked body of light. Perhaps this is how our depressed heads can see hope.

FATHER: But we are not makers of the wardrobe of the universe, son. We are just ordinary slaves to these garments of light and dark.

BOY: We do not need to know how to make these garments, father. Perhaps this is not our duty. Perhaps our obligation is merely to get dressed and undressed.

FATHER: I do not know. I simply do not know.

BOY: Have we made progress, father?

FATHER: We have made progress with our heads, but we were derailed somewhere, son. Let us turn back to the beginning. We sat down because of balance.

BOY: There is sweat, stone, and water.

FATHER: Yes, we must find proper exchanges for them amongst us and redistribute.

BOY: We are terribly lost, father.

FATHER: We are. We are quite lost.

BOY: Will it shatter the fragility of your notion of balance if we estimate, father? Does the weight distribution have to be precise?

FATHER: It has to be an equal and exact exchange, son. The digital scale is here to guarantee precision.

BOY: But it is impossible to be precise, father.

FATHER: It is not impossible, son. You must remember how many little sips and how many big sips you took from my canteen. If you are able to remember, we can re-trace your gesture by performing the sip without you swallowing. You will spit out the little sips and big sips into a cup and I can measure the weight of your sips. To exchange, we will find a rock that will carry the same weight as the weight of your sips.

BOY: Father, I do not remember how many sips, little or big, I have taken.

FATHER: Think, son. Retrace your footsteps.

BOY: But father, you said the solution lies near the future. You have informed me that we must gaze forward. There is nothing in the past for us.

FATHER: I did say this, son. You have found words and logic to cancel out all of my possible solutions. I do not know how to think forward in anticipation.

BOY: Perhaps your thinking at the very beginning was flawed.

FATHER: Perhaps it was. But I have studied this theory for a decade now, son. And it must have some grounds for me to continue to pursue it as I have.

BOY: Father, I think you must abandon what does not work.

FATHER: I do not know if it does or does not work. I must not lose hope in this. We must continue to sit here and think.

BOY: But, father, thinking has not helped us.

FATHER: I suspect this is the case.

BOY: Father, then what must we do next that could be clear to us?

FATHER: What is clear to us, son?

BOY: That we must abandon what is no longer working, father.

FATHER: But something is working or we would not be here.

BOY: Father, there is another fallacy to the calculation and balance situation.

FATHER: What fallacy?

BOY: You said to perform the sip without me swallowing the water, father. You suggested that I spit out the little sips and big sips into a cup so that we could measure the weight of my sips. But some water would be lost in that exchange. My tongue and some part of my mouth would have taken some of the water in my effort to sip and my effort to pretend to swallow. How would we measure how much water had remained in my mouth and how much water had left my mouth?

FATHER: I did say that, but I do not think it is possible now.

BOY: Are you giving up, father?

FATHER: Maybe a little.

BOY: That is a lot, father. A little is a lot in the long run.

FATHER: What do you expect me to do?

BOY: Let us go home, father.

FATHER: That is not a possibility, son.

BOY: What is a possibility then, father?

FATHER: Let us sit here and think a little longer. I do not want
the mountain to think that we have forgotten her.

BOY: Have you lost your memory, father?

FATHER: I have lost something along the way.

BOY: Perhaps you have lost your mind, father. No matter what
we do, we cannot retrieve that.

FATHER: I want to climb the mountain with you, son. So if I
lose my mind in doing so, it is worth it to me. I am
getting so old now.

BOY: You could collapse anytime, father.

FATHER: At any moment.

BOY: Why do you want to see the mountain so badly, father?

FATHER: I do not know, son. It is your thirteenth birthday. Your mother and I had you when we were so old. I thought if I climb with my son I would feel younger.

BOY: That is unstable logic, father.

FATHER: It has become clear to me that it is getting more unstable every moment.

BOY: Your reasoning keeps on changing too, father. First, you want the mountain to think we have not forgotten her. Then you were trying to idealize balance through water calculation. Now, your logic is that we climb because you want to feel younger.

FATHER: I know my desire runs swiftly like a bird. I also thought that if we climb together, my son would become my friend, someone I can walk the path of life with besides your mother. And since your mother is gone—I miss having a friend.

BOY: Father, you are so clumsy with your desire.

FATHER: Is your desire clumsy too, son?

BOY: No, father.

FATHER: What is your desire?

BOY: I do not have desire yet, father.

FATHER: You are at an age to want shapes and things.

BOY: Father, shapes and things.

FATHER: And curves. Do you want curves?

BOY: No, father. I am not drawn to geometry.

FATHER: What are you drawn to?

BOY: I do not know, father. Do I not have my whole life to figure this out?

FATHER: I hope you are drawn to curves, or else your life would be very flat.

BOY: What is wrong with a flat life, father?

FATHER: Nothing is wrong with that. It is just that a curvy life, like the one the mountain has, is far more superior.

BOY: I do not think so, father. All facets of life are worth the same.

FATHER: Nonsense, son. When a storm passes through you, son, you will know what it is like to be in possession of curves.

BOY: If you say so, father.

FATHER: I believe so.

BOY: What will we do now?

FATHER: Now that we have reached a cul-de-sac?

BOY: Yes.

FATHER: If we abandon the balance theory, shall we climb?

BOY: Yes, we shall climb, father.

FATHER: I just have a bad feeling that we should not abandon
that balance theory. I just have a bad feeling. The balance theory is necessary. But I am stumped!

BOY: Perhaps we should not go on, father.

FATHER: Perhaps so.

[Father inserts our canteens into his backpack.]

BOY: Shall we get going, father?

FATHER: Yes, let us. The sun is going to greet us soon.

BOY: And we will not be in the dark anymore, father.

FATHER: I can see your face now.

BOY: I cannot see yours, father. Your face is a bag of black rice.
If you spill over, I would not be able to hold it together.

FATHER: It is strange that you say that. It is strange that I can
see your face, but you cannot see my face.

BOY: Why is that, father?

FATHER: Before you were born, your mother thought I was a
bag of black rice too.

BOY: Father, that is something.

FATHER: I think this time around…when you say what you just
said, it means death's hat covers my face.

BOY: Do not say unnecessary things like that, father.

FATHER: There is the sun, son. Just peeking through the back
of the mountain.

BOY: Indeed, father.

FATHER: I can see your face, bright and crisp, son.

BOY: I cannot see your face, father.

FATHER: That is impossible, son. I have a face. I woke up this
morning with one. And I am still standing here with
one.

[Father reaches up to touch his face.]

BOY: Is it still there, father?

FATHER: Still there, son.

BOY: May I touch it, father?

FATHER: Of course.

[Father lowers his head. I touch it. I feel nothing. As if his face
has been blown out of chaos and become part of the circumfer-
ence of air.]

BOY: I do not feel your face, father.

FATHER: I did not shave this morning...I have stubble from
the evening before. Touch here.

[I touch his chin.]

BOY: Nothing, father. I do not feel anything.

FATHER: That is vexing.

BOY: Indeed, father.

FATHER: I suppose it is not important to have a visible face in order to climb a mountain.

BOY: I guess it is not that important.

FATHER: What is important then, son?

BOY: That we climb.

FATHER: Climb, we must.

[I do not know how far we ascend, but we are ascending at a slow, methodical rate. My faceless father and I are not breathless when we take our time to climb up. I can hear his breathing; it moves softly like mother's dress. I can hear my own breath, breathful and youthful. I climb behind father. He has tall and long legs. Sometimes I feel like a twig before a tree branch. I am not any shorter than my father, but my father is at a higher elevation than me. It gives the illusion that he is a lot taller. We climb and we climb. Father and I cease talking to each other. We are trying to avoid the attention of the morning sun. Our bodies bend toward the body of the mountain. We climb the mountain in a circular fashion. When we are in front of the mountain, the sun is away from us. Then, shadow walks shadow. That is the gesture of our climbing bodies. One foot forward. Mindlessly, the body's motto to itself.]

FATHER: Shall we rest here, son?

BOY: Yes, let us, father.

FATHER: Would you like a sip of water?

BOY: Yes, father.

[Father takes out his canteen from his bag. He unscrews the cap and offers me the canteen. The water tastes young and sweet. I count three small sips and take another three larger sips. I hand the canteen back to father. Father lifts it up and takes several noisy liquid gulps.]

BOY: I took a total of six sips; three smaller ones, three larger ones.

FATHER: That is good. But my son, why do you count when it is no longer necessary?

BOY: I thought you might like to know, father.

FATHER: For what reason, son?

BOY: For no reason, father.

FATHER: What will I do with that knowledge?

BOY: Father, you can tuck it away like a pair of socks in a sock drawer.

FATHER: Yes, I suppose that is the case.

BOY: Perhaps, father. Someone else has to make that sacrifice.

FATHER: Yes, I am afraid someone else had to make that sacrifice, son.

BOY: More than once, father.

FATHER: More than once.

BOY: Possibly multiple people, father.

FATHER: Possibly multiple people.

BOY: That seems so unfair, father.

FATHER: Yes. It seems that way. Is it not strange, son, that a heart is a shatterable entity? And sounds like glass, but is not glass? It can be broken once and it can be broken again.

BOY: My heart is a book, father. It is not made of glass. If someone breaks my heart, it would seem that a page is torn out of me.

FATHER: How many pages is your book, son?

BOY: Three hundred and seventy-two pages, father.

FATHER: Your heart is of a decent thickness.

BOY: My heart is a hardcover, father.

FATHER: Not paperback.

BOY: Father, the first page is the hardest to tear. I imagine. It is the front cover.

FATHER: After that.

BOY: After that, it is easily torn apart, father. One page follows another page.

FATHER: Well, you are still young and you still have a full book.

BOY: No, father.

FATHER: No?

BOY: My front cover is torn off already, father.

FATHER: When did you allow that to happen?

BOY: It happened to me, father. I had no choice.

FATHER: You must be in a great deal of pain.

BOY: Yes, father.

FATHER: Have I met this girl?

BOY: Why do you assume it is a girl, father?

FATHER: Perhaps I should not have made that assumption. Have I met this boy?

BOY: When mother died, she took my front cover with her.

FATHER: Oh, son.

BOY: I know, father.

FATHER: It must be nice. The heart has a title page.

BOY: And numbered pages, father.

FATHER: Have you asked her for it back?

BOY: I do not want it back, father. On windy days, the pages in me lift. I feel myself rustling. Had I known this feeling of aliveness, I wish I had been born with the cover off.

FATHER: Your mother would have died before you were even born.

BOY: This is true, father. I would not want mother dead simply because I want my heart to rustle.

FATHER: Certainly not, son.

BOY: I miss her a great deal, father.

FATHER: I miss her very much too, son.

BOY: I have a feeling you will see her soon, father.

FATHER: I have the same feeling too, son. What will you do?

BOY: I have no clue yet, father.

FATHER: All eight of the bookshelves and the books are yours.

BOY: I know, father.

FATHER: Your mother's earrings are yours, too, son.

BOY: I do not want to be a drag queen, father.

FATHER: I know.

BOY: I do not have to be, father.

FATHER: Perhaps you will be.

BOY: Probably not, father.

FATHER: Your mother's linen sheets—they are yours now.

BOY: Yes, father.

FATHER: My bicycle—the one I rode with you across Morocco—it is yours too.

BOY: I know, father.

FATHER: Your great-great-grandmother's dresser, the one with stone turquoise knobs, it is yours now.

BOY: Yes, father.

FATHER: Your mother's piano—it is yours now too. You must find another piano teacher.

BOY: Yes, father.

FATHER: The polyester hammock with the wooden suspenders—it is now yours as well, son.

BOY: I know, father.

FATHER: I used to hold you in my arms and rock you to sleep while your mother baked key lime pie. At first, I thought your cheeks were a bakery—because you smelled so fresh—especially after your mother bathed you. But it was your mother's key lime pie that had me.

BOY: Yes, that I have not forgotten, father.

FATHER: The Swiss Army knife in the second drawer near the
kitchen sink—from your grandfather to me when I
was just barely eight—that is yours now. Do not let
anyone take that away from you.

BOY: I will not allow it, father.

FATHER: Your mother's purple shawl—wrap it around you
when winter comes. I won't be able to share this winter with you. So cover your body as if I were there.

BOY: I know, father. This winter I will be alone with the snow.

[Father takes out a handkerchief from his hiking pants' pocket
and hands it to me.]

FATHER: My handkerchief for you. Happy thirteenth birthday,
son.

BOY: Thank you, father.

FATHER: So, I must go now, son. I must lean into the mountain so that death can steal my faceless face from me.
When I lean into the mountain it will be as if I am
leaning back into your mother's face. To be with her
once again.

BOY: Yes, father.

FATHER: Does this overwhelm you, son?

BOY: No, father, no. Not yet.

FATHER: Have I missed anything, son?

BOY: No, I do not think so, father.

FATHER: You must remember to take me up the mountain, son.

BOY: Yes, father, I will remember.

FATHER: Goodbye, son.

BOY: Goodbye, father.

[Father quietly leans into the mountain, closes his eyes, and the sun passes over his face like a cloud over a drop of rain. I sit with father in the light. When light bends, father's faceless face perforates and grows transparent against the side of the mountain. It is difficult to determine when father passes away. When his last breath is. It is there one moment and gone the next. I sit there with him. Because he has passed away, his face reappears again like a painted canvas of someone's face, a face that is his, but not his at the same time, wrapped around the mountain. His cheeks are grave and the vibrant colors have drained out, as if his face died several days ago. His presence seems hollowed out. I do not know what to do with myself. It is only seven in the morning. Not long ago the sun greeted my father and me. I couldn't see his face then. And now that I see his face, I do not know what to do with it.]

[I must drag my father's body up the mountain. I stand up, lifting him by the shoulder part of his shirt. In death, father has gained weight. I pull at his sleeves. He is tall and skinny, but he is so heavy. Father, what did you eat? I place his hand over my shoulder and pull him up, but he is just too much. I unwind his hand from my body and study the surface of the cloud. On my thirteenth birthday, my father has given me a lot of gifts. Eight bookshelves, one bicycle, and other things all unwrapped at home. My father leans against the mountain like a shadow from a tree. I pull him by the arms. Then I pull him over to remove his backpack off of him. Then I lean him back against the mountain and lift his arms up. I am afraid if I pull hard enough, I will remove his arm a little away from his body. I pull him up with all my might. He leans into my body like a heavy refrigerator. I make half a yard of progress and then drop his arms and put him down. He crumples down against the mountain like an empty sack of rice. I walk to his backpack. On the side of the mountain, I remove a tarp out of the bag and roll him into it. I thought it would make him lighter, but he just gets heavier. I have to be careful how much I pull. If I pull too hard, I may end up with an empty tarp and my father rolling off the mountain without me. I do not want to say: there goes father. Slowly I discard the unnecessary items—items such as a flashlight, his sleeping bag, and mosquito net—from his bag. I make a few steps forward just to take a few steps backward to retrieve his backpack. Carrying my own backpack is already difficult; I do not want to have to carry two. Taking a rope out of my father's bag, I untwine it. Then I slip underneath his tarp and tie a knot around the tarp and then around his body. He looks like a lettuce-less burrito. Poor father. This will prevent father from slipping down.

Father, I do not want you to die falling to the side of the mountain. I do not want time and rain and weather to petrify you. I do not want you to be part of the mountain. At least let me carry you up so that I can toss you down. You flesh has more meaning at the foot of the mountain than on the side of the mountain. If you are on the side of the mountain, you might rotate. And then I would not know where you will be. But if you are at the foot, then I could always step on you and I would always know where you are. Always beneath me, watching the progress of my life beneath my feet. But, father, please do not drift too far away from the mountain; I would not know where to step on you.]

[The leaves twirl in circles because of the wind. It startles me because I believe the leaves have the motion of bicycle wheels as they mount the mountain.]

[I sit with father in his tarp form. I lean against the mountain hoping to die the way father died, but the mountain will not allow my face to have the same calling as father's. I suspect death is a pancake timer. If the timer on the pancake does not go off, then death cannot flip over and negate me.]

BOY: Father, forgive me for eating your last morsel of bread. I could not wait any longer. I was so hungry. I was going to save it as an oblation when I had lifted you at the top, but my body is growing so weak. I made a simple, but not too difficult choice. To eat my oblation or to have the vigor to take you up the mountain. I chose the second one. I hope you are not displeased.

BOY: Father, I do not know if I have the strength to carry you up the mountain.

BOY: Father! My heart. Why does it feel heavy?

BOY: Father, I do not like this life any more.

BOY: Father, I do not want the hammock. Please come back.

BOY: Father, did you not break a chair instead of dying?

BOY: Father, how is mother? Is she doing okay on the other side of the wall?

BOY: Father, why have you stopped responding?

BOY: Father, the sun is burning so brightly. Each new second into my life, I feel an invisible hand is turning one page of my heart.

BOY: Father, what is it like to return to dust? Is it like life with more red earth?

BOY: Father, I am keeping your digital scale.

BOY: Father, I am sorry I tried to force logic into your intuition.

BOY: Father, I wish I could make you accountable for your wisdom.

BOY: Father, I weighed one sip of water for you.

BOY: Father, would you like to know how much it weighed?

BOY: Father, what would you like to happen to you when I get your body up the mountain?

BOY: Father, I have a feeling I must get rid of everything including the digital scale to get you up there.

BOY: Father, do you still want to be there?

BOY: Father, I tossed your digital scale away because it was getting so heavy.

BOY: Father, tell me more glamorous stories about mother.

BOY: Father, I am drinking all of your water.

BOY: Father, I wish I had some lip balm. Your lips are crackling.

BOY: Father, is there still music left in your lungs?

BOY: Father, I am pressing my ears to your chest to listen to the piano keys of your ribs! Breath is not moving its hands. The music has stopped.

BOY: Father, I lied about fishing with Derek. He just wanted to show me his stepmother's naked pictures.

BOY: Father, forgive me for being so naughty so early in life.

BOY: Father, how will I get you home?

BOY: Father, we have not finished Thomas Mann's book yet. The mountain one. You said it would be over my head and you said you would explain things to me. Let us go home and read it, father.

BOY: Father, where are you?

BOY: Father, it is just me now. I have the whole world to me and no mother and no father.

BOY: Father, what does God smell like?

BOY: Father, why do you just lie there like you are dead?

BOY: Father, my seventh grade teacher likes you so much.

BOY: Father, it is not dark yet. But I know it will get dark and get very lonely. So lonely, father. What will I do then?

BOY: Father, are you lonely too? Have you found mother yet?

BOY: Father, it is so cruel of you to leave me in complete darkness.

BOY: Father—

[I stand up and drag father up the mountain. I work methodically and carefully. Father must not have liked the distribution of his weight. Father folds his body as I drag him up. When he folds his body, his head collapses onto his feet. When he collapses like that, he becomes an awkward ball. Before I can catch him, he tumbles down the mountain like a tumbleweed. I watch father twirl and twist and descend. Poor father, so circular and destroyed in motion.]

BOY: Father!